Our Boys

Entertaining Stories by Popular Authors

Edgard Monette

The Cat-tail Arrow

BY CLARA DOTY BATES

Little Sammie made a bow,
    Well indeed he loved to whittle,
Shaped it like the half of O—
How he could I scarcely know,
    For his fingers were so little.
As he whittled came a sigh:
    "If I only had an arrow;
Something light enough to fly
To the tree-tops or the sky!
    Then I'd have such fun tomorrow."

Then he thought of all the slim
    Things that grow—the hazel bushes,
Willow branches, poplars trim—
And yet nothing suited him
    Till he chanced to think of rushes.
He knew well a quiet pool
    Where he always paused a minute
On his way to district school,
Just to see the waters cool
    And his own bright face within it.

There the cat-tails thickly grew,
    With their heads so brown and furry;
They were straight and slender too,
Plenty strong enough he knew,
    And he sought them in a hurry.
Such an arrow as he wrought—
    Almost passed a boy's believing.
When he drew the bow-string taut,

Out of sight and quick as thought
    Up it went, the blue air cleaving.

Who was Sammie, would you know?
    It was grandpa—he was little
Nearly eighty years ago;
But 'tis no doubt as fine a bow
    As the best he still could whittle.

A YOUNG SALT.

HE COULDN'T SAY NO.

It was sad and it was strange!
   He just was full of knowledge,
His studies swept the whole broad range
   Of High School and of College;
He read in Greek and Latin too,
   Loud Sanscrit he could utter,
      But one small thing he couldn't do
      That comes as pat to me and you
   As eating bread and butter:
He couldn't say "No!" He couldn't say "No!"
I'm sorry to say it was really so!
He'd diddle, and dawdle, and stutter, but oh!
When it came to the point he could never say "No!"

   Geometry he knew by rote,
      Like any Harvard Proctor;
   He'd sing a fugue out, note by note;
      Knew Physics like a Doctor;
   He spoke in German and in French;
      Knew each Botanic table;
         But one small word that you'll agree
         Comes pat enough to you and me,
      To speak he was not able:
For he couldn't say "No!" He couldn't say "No!"
'Tis dreadful, of course, but 'twas really so.
He'd diddle, and dawdle, and stutter, but oh!
When it came to the point he could never say "No!"

   And he could fence, and swim, and float,
      And use the gloves with ease too,
   Could play base ball, and row a boat,
      And hang on a trapeze too;

His temper was beyond rebuke,
    And nothing made him lose it;
        His strength was something quite superb,
        But what's the use of having nerve
    If one can never use it?
He couldn't say "No!" He couldn't say "No!"
If one asked him to come, if one asked him to go,
He'd diddle, and dawdle, and stutter, but oh!
When it came to the point he could never say "No!"

When he was but a little lad,
    In life's small ways progressing,
He fell into this habit bad
    Of always acquiescing;
'Twas such an amiable trait,
    To friend as well as stranger,
        That half unconsciously at last
        The custom held him hard and fast
    Before he knew the danger,
And he couldn't say "No!" He couldn't say "No!"
To his prospects you see 'twas a terrible blow.
He'd diddle, and dawdle, and stutter, but oh!
When it came to the point he could never say "No!"

And so for all his weary days
    The best of chances failed him;
He lived in strange and troublous ways
    And never knew what ailed him;
He'd go to skate when ice was thin;
    He'd join in deeds unlawful,
        He'd lend his name to worthless notes,
        He'd speculate in stocks and oats;
    'Twas positively awful,
For he couldn't say "No!" He couldn't say "No!"
He would veer like a weather-cock turning so slow;
He'd diddle, and dawdle, and stutter, but oh!
When it came to the point he could never say "No!"

Then boys and girls who hear my song,

Pray heed its theme alarming:
Be good, be wise, be kind, be strong—
These traits are always charming,
But all your learning, all your skill
With well-trained brain and muscle,
Might just as well be left alone,
If you can't cultivate backbone
To help you in life's tussle,
And learn to say "No!" Yes, learn to say "No!"
Or you'll fall from the heights to the rapids below!
You may waver, and falter, and tremble, but oh!
When your conscience requires it, be sure and shout "No!"

M.E.B.

THE CHRISTMAS MONKS.

All children have wondered unceasingly from their very first Christmas up to their very last Christmas, where the Christmas presents come from. It is very easy to say that Santa Claus brought them. All well regulated people know that, of course; about the reindeer, and the sledge, and the pack crammed with toys, the chimney, and all the rest of it—that is all true, of course, and everybody knows about it; but that is not the question which puzzles. What children want to know is, where do these Christmas presents come from in the first place? Where does Santa Claus get them? Well, the answer to that is, *In the garden of the Christmas Monks*. This has not been known until very lately; that is, it has not been known till very lately except in the immediate vicinity of the Christmas Monks. There, of course, it has been known for ages. It is rather an out-of-the-way place; and that accounts for our never hearing of it before.

The Convent of the Christmas Monks is a most charmingly picturesque pile of old buildings; there are towers and turrets, and peaked roofs and arches, and everything which could possibly be thought of in the architectural line, to make a convent picturesque. It is built of graystone; but it is only once in a while that you can see the graystone, for the walls are almost completely covered with mistletoe and ivy and evergreen. There are the most delicious little arched windows with diamond panes peeping out from the mistletoe and evergreen, and always at all times of the year, a little Christmas wreath of ivy and holly-berries is suspended in the centre of every window. Over all the doors, which are likewise arched, are Christmas garlands, and over the main entrance *MerryChristmas* in evergreen letters.

The Christmas Monks are a jolly brethren; the robes of their order are white, gilded with green garlands, and they never are seen out at any time of the year without Christmas wreaths on their heads. Every morning they file in a long procession into the chapel to sing a Christmas carol; and every evening they ring a Christmas chime on the convent bells. They eat roast turkey and plum pudding and mince-pie for dinner all the year round; and always carry what is left in baskets trimmed with evergreen to the poor people. There are always wax candles lighted and set in every window of the convent at nightfall; and when the people in the country about get uncommonly blue and down-hearted, they always go for a cure to look at the Convent of the Christmas Monks after the candles are lighted and the chimes are ringing. It brings to mind things which never fail to cheer them.

But the principal thing about the Convent of the Christmas Monks is the garden; for that is where the Christmas presents grow. This garden extends over a large number of acres, and is divided into different departments, just as we divide our flower and vegetable gardens; one bed for onions, one for cabbages, and one for phlox, and one for verbenas, etc.

Every spring the Christmas Monks go out to sow the Christmas-present seeds after they have ploughed the ground and made it all ready.

There is one enormous bed devoted to rocking-horses. The rocking-horse seed is curious enough; just little bits of rocking-horses so small that they can only be seen through a very, very powerful microscope. The Monks drop these at quite a distance from each other, so that they will not interfere while growing; then they cover them up neatly with earth, and put up a sign-post with "Rocking-horses" on it in evergreen letters. Just so with the penny-trumpet seed, and the toy-furniture seed, the skate-seed, the sled-seed, and all the others.

Perhaps the prettiest, and most interesting part of the garden, is that devoted to wax dolls. There are other beds for the commoner dolls—for the rag dolls, and the china dolls, and the rubber dolls, but of course wax dolls would look much handsomer growing. Wax dolls have to be planted quite early in the season; for they need a good start before the sun is very high. The seeds are the loveliest bits of microscopic dolls imaginable. The Monks sow them pretty close together, and they begin to come up by the middle of May. There is first just a little glimmer of gold, or flaxen, or black, or brown, as the case may be, above the soil. Then the snowy foreheads appear, and the blue eyes, and the black eyes, and, later on, all those enchanting little heads are out of the ground, and are nodding and winking and smiling to each other the whole extent of the field; with their pinky cheeks and sparkling eyes and curly hair there is nothing so pretty as these little wax doll heads peeping out of the earth.

Gradually, more and more of them come to light, and finally by Christmas they are all ready to gather. There they stand, swaying to and fro, and dancing lightly on their slender feet which are connected with the ground, each by a tiny green stem; their dresses of pink, or blue, or white—for their dresses grow with them—flutter in the air. Just about the prettiest sight in the world is the bed of wax dolls in the garden of the Christmas Monks at Christmas time. Of course ever since this convent and garden were established (and that was so long ago that the wisest man can find no books about it) their glories have attracted a vast deal of admiration and curiosity from the young people in the surrounding country; but as the garden is enclosed on all sides by an immensely thick and high hedge, which no boy could climb, or peep over, they could only judge of the garden by the fruits which were parceled out to them on Christmas-day.

You can judge, then, of the sensation among the young folks, and older ones, for that matter, when one evening there appeared hung upon a conspicuous place in the garden-hedge, a broad strip of white cloth trimmed with evergreen and printed with the following notice in evergreen letters:

"WANTED—By the Christmas Monks, two *good* boys to assist in garden work. Applicants will be examined by Fathers Anselmus and Ambrose, in the convent refectory, on April 10th."

This notice was hung out about five o'clock in the evening, some time in the early part of February. By noon the street was so full of boys staring at it with their mouths wide open, so as to see better, that the king was obliged to send his bodyguard before him to clear the way with brooms, when he wanted to pass on his way from his chamber of state to his palace.

There was not a boy in the country but looked upon this position as the height of human felicity. To work all the year in that wonderful garden, and see those wonderful things growing! and without doubt any body who worked there could have all the toys he wanted, just as a boy who works in a candy-shop always has all the candy he wants!

But the great difficulty, of course, was about the degree of goodness requisite to pass the examination. The boys in this country were no worse than the boys in other countries, but there were not many of them that would not have done a little differently if he had only known beforehand of the advertisement of the

Christmas Monks. However, they made the most of the time remaining, and were so good all over the kingdom that a very millennium seemed dawning. The school teachers used their ferrules for fire wood, and the king ordered all the birch trees cut down and exported, as he thought there would be no more call for them in his own realm.

When the time for the examination drew near, there were two boys whom every one thought would obtain the situation, although some of the other boys had lingering hopes for themselves; if only the Monks would examine them on the last six weeks, they thought they might pass. Still all the older people had decided in their minds that the Monks would choose these two boys. One was the Prince, the king's oldest son; and the other was a poor boy named Peter. The Prince was no better than the other boys; indeed, to tell the truth, he was not so good; in fact, was the biggest rogue in the whole country; but all the lords and the ladies, and all the people who admired the lords and ladies, said it was their solemn belief that the Prince was the best boy in the whole kingdom; and they were prepared to give in their testimony, one and all, to that effect to the Christmas Monks.

Peter was really and truly such a good boy that there was no excuse for saying he was not. His father and mother were poor people; and Peter worked every minute out of school hours to help them along. Then he had a sweet little crippled sister whom he was never tired of caring for. Then, too, he contrived to find time to do lots of little kindnesses for other people. He always studied his lessons faithfully, and never ran away from school. Peter was such a good boy, and so modest and unsuspicious that he was good, that everybody loved him. He had not the least idea that he could get the place with the Christmas Monks, but the Prince was sure of it.

When the examination day came all the boys from far and near, with their hair neatly brushed and parted, and dressed in their best clothes, flocked into the convent. Many of their relatives and friends went with them to witness the examination.

The refectory of the convent, where they assembled, was a very large hall with a delicious smell of roast turkey and plum pudding in it. All the little boys sniffed, and their mouths watered.

The two fathers who were to examine the boys were perched up in a high pulpit so profusely trimmed with evergreen that it looked like a bird's nest; they were remarkably pleasant-looking men, and their eyes twinkled merrily under their Christmas wreaths. Father Anselmus was a little the taller of the two, and Father Ambrose was a little the broader; and that was about all the difference between them in looks.

THE PRINCE &
PETER ARE EXAMINED
BY THE MONKS.

The little boys all stood up in a row, their friends stationed themselves in good places, and the examination began.

Then if one had been placed beside the entrance to the convent, he would have seen one after another, a crestfallen little boy with his arm lifted up and crooked, and his face hidden in it, come out and walk forlornly away. He had failed to pass.

The two fathers found out that this boy had robbed birds' nests, and this one stolen apples. And one after another they walked disconsolately away till there were only two boys left: the Prince and Peter.

"Now, your Highness," said Father Anselmus, who always took the lead in the questions, "are you a good boy?"

"O holy Father!" exclaimed all the people—there were a good many fine folks from the court present. "He is such a good boy! such a wonderful boy! We never knew him to do a wrong thing in his sweet life."

"I don't suppose he ever robbed a bird's nest?" said Father Ambrose a little doubtfully.

"No, no!" chorused the people.

"Nor tormented a kitten?"

"No, no, no!" cried they all.

At last everybody being so confident that here could be no reasonable fault found with the Prince, he was pronounced competent to enter upon the Monks' service. Peter they knew a great deal about before—indeed, a glance at his face was enough to satisfy any one of his goodness; for he did look more like one of the boy angels in the altar-piece than anything else. So after a few questions, they accepted him also; and the people went home and left the two boys with the Christmas Monks.

The next morning Peter was obliged to lay aside his homespun coat, and the Prince his velvet tunic, and both were dressed in some little white robes with evergreen girdles like the Monks. Then the Prince was set to sowing Noah's ark seed, and Peter picture-book seed. Up and down they went scattering the seed. Peter sang a little psalm to himself, but the Prince grumbled because they had not given him gold-watch or gem seed to plant instead of the toy which he had outgrown long ago. By noon Peter had planted all his picture-books, and fastened up the card to mark them on the pole; but the Prince had dawdled so his work was not half done.

"We are going to have a trial with this boy," said the Monks to each other; "we shall have to set him a penance at once, or we cannot manage him at all."

So the Prince had to go without his dinner, and kneel on dried peas in the chapel all the afternoon. The next day he finished his Noah's Arks meekly; but the next day he rebelled again and had to go the whole length of the field where they planted jewsharps, on his knees. And so it was about every other day for the whole year.

One of the brothers had to be set apart in a meditating cell to invent new penances; for they had used up all on their list before the Prince had been with them three months.

The Prince became dreadfully tired of his convent life, and if he could have brought it about would have run away. Peter, on the contrary, had never been so happy in his life. He worked like a bee, and the pleasure he took in seeing the lovely things he had planted come up, was unbounded, and the Christmas carols and chimes delighted his soul. Then, too, he had never fared so well in his life. He could never remember the time before when he had been a whole week without being hungry. He sent his wages every month to his parents; and he never ceased to wonder at the discontent of the Prince.

"They grow so slow," the Prince would say, wrinkling up his handsome forehead. "I expected to have a bushelful of new toys every month; and not one have I had yet. And these stingy old Monks say I can only have my usual Christmas share anyway, nor can I pick them out myself. I never saw such a stupid place to stay in my life. I want to have my velvet tunic on and go home to the palace and ride on my white pony with the silver tail, and hear them all tell me how charming I am." Then the Prince would crook his arm and put his head on it and cry.

Peter pitied him, and tried to comfort him, but it was not of much use, for the Prince got angry because he was not discontented as well as himself.

Two weeks before Christmas everything in the garden was nearly ready to be picked. Some few things needed a little more December sun, but everything looked perfect. Some of the Jack-in-the-boxes would not pop out quite quick enough, and some of the jumping-Jacks were hardly as limber as they might be as yet; that was all. As it was so near Christmas the Monks were engaged in their holy exercises in the chapel for the greater part of the time, and only went over the garden once a day to see if everything was all right.

The Prince and Peter were obliged to be there all the time. There was plenty of work for them to do; for once in a while something would blow over, and then there were the penny-trumpets to keep in tune; and that was a vast sight of work.

One morning the Prince was at one end of the garden straightening up some wooden soldiers which had toppled over, and Peter was in the wax doll bed dusting the dolls. All of a sudden he heard a sweet little voice: "O, Peter!" He thought at first one of the dolls was talking, but they could not say anything but papa and mamma; and had the merest apologies for voices anyway. "Here I am, Peter!" and there was a little pull at his sleeve. There was his little sister. She was not any taller than the dolls around her, and looked uncommonly like the prettiest, pinkest-cheeked, yellowest-haired ones; so it was no wonder that Peter did not see her at first. She stood there poising herself on her crutches, poor little thing, and smiling lovingly up at Peter.

"Oh, you darling!" cried Peter, catching her up in his arms. "How did you get in here?"

"I stole in behind one of the Monks," said she. "I saw him going up the street past our house, and I ran out and kept behind him all the way. When he opened the gate I whisked in too, and then I followed him into the garden. I've been here with the dollies ever since."

"Well," said poor Peter, "I don't see what I am going to do with you, now you are here. I can't let you out again; and I don't know what the Monks will say."

"Oh, I know!" cried the little girl gayly. "I'll stay out here in the garden. I can sleep in one of those beautiful dolls' cradles over there; and you can bring me something to eat."

THE BOYS AT
WORK IN
THE
CONVENT
GARDEN.

"But the Monks come out every morning to look over the garden, and they'll be sure to find you," said her brother, anxiously.

"No, I'll hide! O Peter, here is a place where there isn't any doll!"

"Yes; that doll did not come up."

"Well, I'll tell you what I'll do! I'll just stand here in this place where the doll didn't come up, and nobody can tell the difference."

"Well, I don't know but you can do that," said Peter, although he was still ill at ease. He was so good a boy he was very much afraid of doing wrong, and offending his kind friends the Monks; at the same time he could not help being glad to see his dear little sister.

He smuggled some food out to her, and she played merrily about him all day; and at night he tucked her into one of the dolls' cradles with lace pillows and quilt of rose-colored silk.

The next morning when the Monks were going the rounds, the father who inspected the wax doll bed was a bit nearsighted, and he never noticed the difference between the dolls and Peter's little sister, who swung herself on her crutches, and looked just as much like a wax doll as she possibly could. So the two were delighted with the success of their plan.

They went on thus for a few days, and Peter could not help being happy with his darling little sister, although at the same time he could not help worrying for fear he was doing wrong.

Something else happened now, which made him worry still more; the Prince ran away. He had been watching for a long time for an opportunity to possess himself of a certain long ladder made of twisted evergreen ropes, which the Monks kept locked up in the toolhouse. Lately, by some oversight, the toolhouse had been left unlocked one day, and the Prince got the ladder. It was the latter part of the afternoon, and the Christmas Monks were all in the chapel practicing Christmas carols. The Prince found a very large hamper, and picked as many Christmas presents for himself as he could stuff into it; then he put the ladder against the high gate in front of the convent, and climbed up, dragging the hamper after him. When he reached the top of the gate, which was quite broad, he sat down to rest for a moment before pulling the ladder up so as to drop it on the other side.

He gave his feet a little triumphant kick as he looked back at his prison, and down slid the evergreen ladder! The Prince lost his balance, and would inevitably have broken his neck if he had not clung desperately to the hamper which hung over on the convent side of the fence; and as it was just the same weight as the Prince, it kept him suspended on the other.

He screamed with all the force of his royal lungs; was heard by a party of noblemen who were galloping up the street; was rescued, and carried in state to the palace. But he was obliged to drop the hamper of presents, for with it all the ingenuity of the noblemen could not rescue him as speedily as it was necessary they should.

When the good Monks discovered the escape of the Prince they were greatly grieved, for they had tried their best to do well by him; and poor Peter could with difficulty be comforted. He had been very fond of the Prince, although the latter had done little except torment him for the whole year; but Peter had a way of being fond of folks.

A few days after the Prince ran away, and the day before the one on which the Christmas presents were to be gathered, the nearsighted father went out into the wax doll field again; but this time he had his spectacles on, and could see just as well as any one, and even a little better. Peter's little sister was swinging herself on her crutches, in the place where the wax doll did not come up, tipping her little face up, and smiling just like the dolls around her.

"Why, what is this!" said the father. "*Hoc credam!* I thought that wax doll did not come up. Can my eyes deceive me? *non verum est!* There is a doll there—and what a doll! on crutches, and in poor, homely gear!"

Then the nearsighted father put out his hand toward Peter's little sister. She jumped—she could not help it, and the holy father jumped too; the Christmas wreath actually tumbled off his head.

"It is a miracle!" exclaimed he when he could speak; "the little girl is alive! *parra puella viva est.* I will pick her and take her to the brethren, and we will pay her the honors she is entitled to."

Then the good father put on his Christmas wreath, for he dare not venture before his abbot without it, picked up Peter's little sister, who was trembling in all her little bones, and carried her into the chapel, where the Monks were just assembling to sing another carol. He went right up to the Christmas abbot, who was seated in a splendid chair, and looked like a king.

"Most holy abbot," said the nearsighted father, holding out Peter's little sister, "behold a miracle, *vide miraculum*! Thou wilt remember that there was one wax doll planted which did not come up. Behold, in her place I have found this doll on crutches, which is—alive!"

"Let me see her!" said the abbot; and all the other Monks crowded around, opening their mouths just like the little boys around the notice, in order to see better.

"*Verumest* ," said the abbot. "It is verily a miracle."

"Rather a lame miracle," said the brother who had charge of the funny picture-books and the toy monkeys; they rather threw his mind off its level of sobriety, and he was apt to make frivolous speeches unbecoming a monk.

The abbot gave him a reproving glance, and the brother, who was the leach of the convent, came forward. "Let me look at the miracle, most holy abbot," said he. He took up Peter's sister, and looked carefully at the small, twisted ankle. "I think I can cure this with my herbs and simples," said he.

"But I don't know," said the abbot doubtfully. "I never heard of curing a miracle."

"If it is not lawful, my humble power will not suffice to cure it," said the father who was the leach.

"True," said the abbot; "take her, then, and exercise thy healing art upon her, and we will go on with our Christmas devotions, for which we should now feel all the more zeal."

So the father took away Peter's little sister, who was still too frightened to speak.

The Christmas Monk was a wonderful doctor, for by Christmas eve the little girl was completely cured of her lameness. This may seem incredible, but it was owing in great part to the herbs and simples, which are of a species that our doctors have no knowledge of; and also to a wonderful lotion which has never been advertised on our fences.

Peter of course heard the talk about the miracle, and knew at once what it meant. He was almost heartbroken to think he was deceiving the Monks so, but at the same time he did not dare to confess the truth for fear they would put a penance upon his sister, and he could not bear to think of her having to kneel upon dried peas.

THE PRINCE RUNS AWAY.

He worked hard picking Christmas presents, and hid his unhappiness as best he could. On Christmas eve he was called into the chapel. The Christmas Monks were all assembled there. The walls were covered with green garlands and boughs and sprays of holly berries, and branches of wax lights Were gleaming brightly amongst them. The altar and the picture of the Blessed Child behind it were so bright as to almost dazzle one; and right up in the midst of it, in a lovely white dress, all wreaths and jewels, in a little chair with a canopy woven of green branches over it, sat Peter's little sister.

And there were all the Christmas Monks in their white robes and wreaths, going up in a long procession, with their hands full of the very showiest Christmas presents to offer them to her!

But when they reached her and held out the lovely presents—the first was an enchanting wax doll, the biggest beauty in the whole garden—instead of reaching out her hands for them, she just drew back, and said in her little sweet, piping voice: "Please, I ain't a millacle, I'm only Peter's little sister."

"Peter?" said the abbot; "the Peter who works in our garden?"

"Yes," said the little sister.

Now here was a fine opportunity for a whole convent full of monks to look foolish—filing up in procession with their hands full of gifts to offer to a miracle, and finding there was no miracle, but only Peter's little sister.

But the abbot of the Christmas Monks had always maintained that there were two ways of looking at all things; if any object was not what you wanted it to be in one light, that there was another light in which it would be sure to meet your views.

So now he brought this philosophy to bear.

"This little girl did not come up in the place of the wax doll, and she is not a miracle in that light," said he; "but look at her in another light and she is a miracle—do you not see?"

They all looked at her, the darling little girl, the very meaning and sweetness of all Christmas in her loving, trusting, innocent face.

"Yes," said all the Christmas Monks, "she is a miracle." And they all laid their beautiful Christmas presents down before her.

Peter was so delighted he hardly knew himself; and, oh! the joy there was when he led his little sister home on Christmas-day, and showed all the wonderful presents.

The Christmas Monks always retained Peter in their employ—in fact he is in their employ to this day. And his parents, and his little sister who was entirely cured of her lameness, have never wanted for anything.

As for the Prince, the courtiers were never tired of discussing and admiring his wonderful knowledge of physics which led to his adjusting the weight of the hamper of Christmas presents to his own so nicely that he could not fall. The Prince liked the talk and the admiration well enough, but he could not help, also, being a little glum; for he got no Christmas presents that year.

MARY E. WILKINS.

TEDDY AND THE ECHO.

Teddy is out upon the lake;
His oars a softened click-clack make;
On all that water bright and blue,
His boat is the only one in view;
So, when he hears another oar
Click-clack along the farthest shore,
"Heigh-ho," he cries, "out for a row!
Echo is out! heigh-ho—heigh-ho!"
　　"Heigh-ho, heigh-ho!"
Sounds from the distance, faint and low.

Then Teddy whistles that he may hear
Her answering whistle, soft and clear;
Out of the greenwood, leafy, mute,
Pipes her mimicking, silver flute,
And, though her mellow measures are
Always behind him half a bar,
'Tis sweet to hear her falter so;
And Ted calls back, "Bravo, bravo!"
　　"Bravo, bravo!"
Comes from the distance, faint and low.

She laughs at trifles loud and long;
Splashes the water, sings a song;
Tells him everything she is told,
Saucy or tender, rough or bold;
One might think from the merry noise
That the quiet wood was full of boys,
Till Ted, grown tired, cries out, "Oh, no!
'Tis dinner time and I must go!"
　　"Must go? must go?"
Sighs from the distance, sad and low.

When Ted and his clatter are away,
Where does the little Echo stay?
Perched on a rock to watch for him?
Or keeping a lookout from some limb?
If he were to push his boat to land,
Would he find her footprint on the sand?
Or would she come to his blithe "hello,"
Red as a rose, or white as snow?
     Ah no, ah no!
Never can Teddy see Echo!

MRS. CLARA DOTY BATES.

SONG OF THE CHRISTMAS STOCKINGS.

Six merry stockings in the firelight,
Hanging by the chimney snug and tight:
      Jolly, jolly red,
      That belongs to Ted;
      Daintiest blue,
      That belongs to Sue;
      Old brown fellow
      Hanging long,
      That belongs to Joe,
      Big and strong;
      Little, wee, pink mite
      Covers Baby's toes—
      Won't she pull it open
      With funny little crows!
      Sober, dark gray,
      Quiet little mouse,
      That belongs to Sybil
      Of all the house;
      One stocking left,
      Whose should it be?
      Why, that I'm sure
      Must belong to me!
Well, so they hang, packed to the brim,
Swing, swing, swing, in the firelight dim.

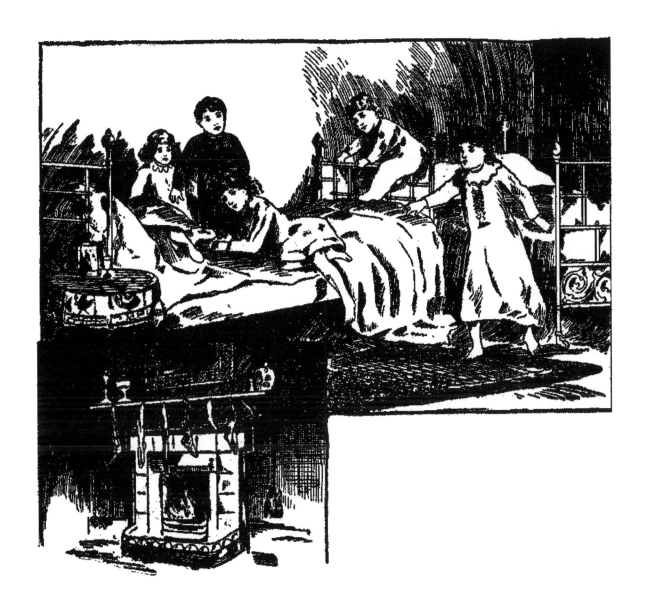

'Twas the middle of the night.
  Open flew my eyes;
 I started up in bed,
  And stared in surprise;
I rubbed my eyes, I rubbed my ears,
I saw the stockings swing, I heard the stockings sing;
    Out in the firelight
    Merry and bright,
    Snug and tight,
    Six were swinging,
    Six were singing,
    Like everything!

And the red, and the blue, and the brown, and the gray,
And the pink one, and mine, had it all their own way,
And no one could stop them—because, don't you see,
Nobody heard 'em—but just poor me!

"All day we carry toes,
    To-night we carry candy;
  Christmas comes once a year
    Very nice and handy.
Run, run, race all day,
Mother mends us after play,
We don't care, life is gay,
Sing and swing, away, away!

"Boots and little tired shoes,
    We kick 'em off in glee;
  It's fun to hang up here
    And Santa Claus to see.
Run, run, race all day,
Mother mends us after play,
We don't care, life is gay,
Sing and swing, away, away!

"To-morrow down we come,
  The sweet things tumble out,
  Then carrying toes again
  We'll have to trot about.
Run, run, race all day,
Mother'll mend us after play,
We don't care, we'll swing so gay
While we can—away, away!"

MARGARET SIDNEY.

JOE LAMBERT'S FERRY.

It was a thoroughly disagreeable March morning. The wind blew in sharp gusts from every quarter of the compass by turns. It seemed to take especial delight in rushing suddenly around corners and taking away the breath of anybody it could catch there coming from the opposite direction. The dust, too, filled people's eyes and noses and mouths, while the damp raw March air easily found its way through the best clothing, and turned boys' skins into pimply goose-flesh.

It was about as disagreeable a morning for going out as can be imagined; and yet everybody in the little Western river town who could get out went out and stayed out.

Men and women, boys and girls, and even little children, ran to the river-bank: and, once there, they stayed, with no thought, it seemed, of going back to their homes or their work.

The people of the town were wild with excitement, and everybody told everybody else what had happened, although everybody knew all about it already. Everybody, I mean, except Joe Lambert, and he had been so busy ever since daylight, sawing wood in Squire Grisard's woodshed, that he had neither seen nor heard anything at all. Joe was the poorest person in the town. He was the only boy there who really had no home and nobody to care for him. Three or four years before this March morning, Joe had been left an orphan, and being utterly destitute, he should have been sent to the poorhouse, or "bound out" to some person as a sort of servant. But Joe Lambert had refused to go to the poorhouse or to become a bound boy. He had declared his ability to take care of himself, and by working hard at odd jobs, sawing wood, rolling barrels on the wharf, picking apples or weeding onions as opportunity offered, he had managed to support himself "after a manner," as the village people said. That is to say, he generally got enough to eat, and some clothes to wear. He slept in a warehouse shed, the owner having given him leave to do so on condition that he would act as a sort of watchman on the premises.

Joe Lambert alone of all the villagers knew nothing of what had happened; and of course Joe Lambert did not count for anything in the estimation of people who had houses to live in. The only reason I have gone out of the way to make an exception of so unimportant a person is, that I think Joe did count for something on that particular March day at least.

When he finished the pile of wood that he had to saw, and went to the house to get his money, he found nobody there. Going down the street he found the town empty, and, looking down a cross street, he saw the crowds that had gathered on the river-bank, thus learning at last that something unusual had occurred. Of course he ran to the river to learn what it was.

When he got there he learned that Noah Martin the fisherman who was also the ferryman between the village and its neighbor on the other side of the river, had been drowned during the early morning in a foolish attempt to row his ferry skiff across the stream. The ice which had blocked the river for two months, had begun to move on the day before, and Martin with his wife and baby—a child about a year old—were on the other side of the river at the time. Early on that morning there had been a temporary gorging of the ice about a mile above the town, and, taking advantage of the comparatively free channel, Martin had tried to cross with his wife and child, in his boat.

The gorge had broken up almost immediately, as the river was rising rapidly, and Martin's boat had been caught and crushed in the ice. Martin had been drowned, but his wife, with her child in her arms, had clung to the wreck of the skiff, and had been carried by the current to a little low-lying island just in front of the town.

What had happened was of less importance, however, than what people saw must happen. The poor woman and baby out there on the island, drenched as they had been in the icy water, must soon die with cold, and, moreover, the island was now nearly under water, while the great stream was rising rapidly. It was evident that within an hour or two the water would sweep over the whole surface of the island, and the great fields of ice would of course carry the woman and child to a terrible death.

Many wild suggestions were made for their rescue, but none that gave the least hope of success. It was simply impossible to launch a boat. The vast fields of ice, two or three feet in thickness, and from twenty feet to a hundred yards in breadth, were crushing and grinding down the river at the rate of four or five miles an hour, turning and twisting about, sometimes jamming their edges together with so great a force that one would lap over another, and sometimes drifting apart and leaving wide open spaces between for a moment or two. One might as well go upon such a river in an egg shell as in the stoutest row-boat ever built.

The poor woman with her babe could be seen from the shore, standing there alone on the rapidly narrowing strip of island. Her voice could not reach the people on the bank, but when she held her poor little baby toward them in mute appeal for help, the mothers there understood her agony.

There was nothing to be done, however. Human sympathy was given freely, but human help was out of the question. Everybody on the river-shore was agreed in that opinion. Everybody, that is to say, except Joe Lambert. He had been so long in the habit of finding ways to help himself under difficulties, that he did not easily make up his mind to think any case hopeless.

No sooner did Joe clearly understand how matters stood than he ran away from the crowd, nobody paying any attention to what he did. Half an hour later somebody cried out: "Look there! Who's that, and what's he going to do?" pointing up the stream.

Looking in that direction, the people saw some one three quarters of a mile away standing on a floating field of ice in the river. He had a large farm-basket strapped upon his shoulders, while in his hands he held a plank.

As the ice-field upon which he stood neared another, the youth ran forward, threw his plank down, making a bridge of it, and crossed to the farther field. Then picking up his plank, he waited for a chance to repeat the process.

As he thus drifted down the river, every eye was strained in his direction. Presently some one cried out: "It's Joe Lambert; and he's trying to cross to the island!"

There was a shout as the people understood the nature of Joe's heroic attempt, and then a hush as its extreme danger became apparent.

Joe had laid his plans wisely and well, but it seemed impossible that he could succeed. His purpose was, with the aid of the plank to cross from one ice-field to another until he should reach the island; but as that would require a good deal of time, and the ice was moving down stream pretty rapidly, it was necessary to start at a point above the town. Joe had gone about a mile up the river before going on the ice, and when first seen from the town he had already reached the channel.

After that first shout a whisper might have been heard in the crowd on the bank. The heroism of the poor boy's attempt awed the spectators, and the momentary expectation that he would disappear forever amid the crushing ice-fields, made them hold their breath in anxiety and terror.

His greatest danger was from the smaller cakes of ice. When it became necessary for him to step upon one of these, his weight was sufficient to make it tilt, and his footing was very insecure. After awhile as he was nearing the island, he came into a large collection of these smaller ice-cakes. For awhile he waited, hoping that a larger field would drift near him; but after a minute's delay he saw that he was rapidly floating past the island, and that he must either trust himself to the treacherous broken ice, or fail in his attempt to save the woman and child.

Choosing the best of the floes, he laid his plank and passed across successfully. In the next passage, however, the cake tilted up, and Joe Lambert went down into the water! A shudder passed through the crowd on shore.

"Poor fellow!" exclaimed some tender-hearted spectator; "it is all over with him now."

"No; look, look!" shouted another. "He's trying to climb upon the ice. Hurrah! he's on his feet again!" With that the whole company of spectators shouted for joy.

Joe had managed to regain his plank as well as to climb upon a cake of ice before the fields around could crush him, and now moving cautiously, he made his way, little by little toward the island.

"Hurrah! Hurrah! he's there at last!" shouted the people on the shore.

"But will he get back again?" was the question each one asked himself a moment later.

Having reached the island, Joe very well knew that the more difficult part of his task was still before him, for it was one thing for an active boy to work his way over floating ice, and quite another to carry a child and lead a woman upon a similar journey.

But Joe Lambert was quick-witted and "long-headed," as well as brave, and he meant to do all that he could to save these poor creatures for whom he had risked his life so heroically. Taking out his knife he made the woman cut her skirts off at the knees, so that she might walk and leap more freely. Then placing the baby in the basket which was strapped upon his back, he cautioned the woman against giving way to fright, and instructed her carefully about the method of crossing.

On the return journey Joe was able to avoid one great risk. As it was not necessary to land at any particular point, time was of little consequence, and hence when no large field of ice was at hand, he could wait for one to approach, without attempting to make use of the smaller ones. Leading the woman wherever that was necessary, he slowly made his way toward shore, drifting down the river, of course, while all the people of the town marched along the bank.

When at last Joe leaped ashore in company with the woman, and bearing her babe in the basket on his back, the people seemed ready to trample upon each other in their eagerness to shake hands with their hero.

Their hero was barely able to stand, however. Drenched as he had been in the icy river, the sharp March wind had chilled him to the marrow, and one of the village doctors speedily lifted him into his carriage which he had brought for that purpose, and drove rapidly away, while the other physician took charge of Mrs. Martin and the baby.

Joe was a strong, healthy fellow, and under the doctor's treatment of hot brandy and vigorous rubbing with coarse towels, he soon warmed. Then he wanted to saw enough wood for the doctor to pay for his treatment, and thereupon the doctor threatened to poison him if he should ever venture to mention pay to him again.

Naturally enough the village people talked of nothing but Joe Lambert's heroic deed, and the feeling was general that they had never done their duty toward the poor orphan boy. There was an eager wish to help him now, and many offers were made to him; but these all took the form of charity, and Joe would not accept charity at all. Four years earlier, as I have already said, he had refused to go to the poorhouse or to be "bound out," declaring that he could take care of himself; and when some thoughtless person had said in his hearing that he would have to live on charity, Joe's reply had been:

"I'll never eat a mouthful in this town that I haven't worked for if I starve." And he had kept his word. Now that he was fifteen years old he was not willing to begin receiving charity even in the form of a reward for his good deed.

One day when some of the most prominent men of the village were talking to him on the subject Joe said:

"I don't want anything except a chance to work, but I'll tell you what you may do for me if you will. Now that poor Martin is dead the ferry privilege will be to lease again, I'd like to get it for a good long term. Maybe I can make something out of it by being always ready to row people across, and I may even be able to put on something better than a skiff after awhile. I'll pay the village what Martin paid."

The gentlemen were glad enough of a chance to do Joe even this small favor, and there was no difficulty in the way. The authorities gladly granted Joe a lease of the ferry privilege for twenty years, at twenty dollars a year rent, which was the rate Martin had paid.

At first Joe rowed people back and forth, saving what money he got very carefully. This was all that could be required of him, but it occurred to Joe that if he had a ferry boat big enough, a good many horses and cattle and a good deal of freight would be sent across the river, for he was a "long-headed" fellow as I have said.

One day a chance offered, and he bought for twenty-five dollars a large old wood boat, which was simply a square barge forty feet long and fifteen feet wide, with bevelled bow and stern, made to hold cord wood for the steamboats. With his own hands he laid a stout deck on this, and, with the assistance of a man whom he hired for that purpose, he constructed a pair of paddle wheels. By that time Joe was out of money, and work on the boat was suspended for awhile. When he had accumulated a little more money, he bought a horse power, and placed it in the middle of his boat, connecting it with the shaft of his wheels. Then he made a rudder and helm, and his horse-boat was ready for use. It had cost him about a hundred dollars besides his own labor upon it, but it would carry live stock and freight as well as passengers, and so the business of the ferry rapidly increased, and Joe began to put a little money away in the bank.

After awhile a railroad was built into the village, and then a second one came. A year later another railroad was opened on the other side of the river, and all the passengers who came to one village by rail had to be ferried across the river in order to continue their journey by the railroads there. The horse-boat was too small and too slow for the business, and Joe Lambert had to buy two steam ferry-boats to take its place. These cost more money than he had, but, as the owner of the ferry privilege, his credit was good, and the boats soon paid for themselves, while Joe's bank account grew again.

Finally the railroad people determined to run through cars for passengers and freight, and to carry them across the river on large boats built for that purpose; but before they gave their orders to their boat builders, they were waited upon by the attorneys of Joe Lambert, who soon convinced them that his ferry privilege gave him alone the right to run any kind of ferry-boats between the two villages which had now grown to such size that they called themselves cities. The result was that the railroads made a contract with Joe to carry their cars across, and he had some large boats built for that purpose.

All this occurred a good many years ago, and Joe Lambert is not called Joe now, but Captain Lambert. He is one of the most prosperous men in the little river city, and owns many large river steamers besides his ferry-boats. Nobody is readier than he to help a poor boy or a poor man; but he has his own way of doing it. He will never toss so much as a cent to a beggar, but he never refuses to give man or boy a chance to earn money by work. He has an odd theory that money which comes without work does more harm than good.

GEORGE CARY EGGLESTON.

THE CHRISTMAS GIFT.

O you dear little dog, all eyes and fluff!
How can I ever love you enough?
How was it, I wonder, that any one knew
I wanted a little dog, just like you?
With your jet black nose, and each sharp-cut ear,
And the tail you wag—O you *are* so dear!
Did you come trotting through all the snow
To find my door, I should like to know?
Or did you ride with the fairy team
Of Santa Claus, of which children dream,
Tucked all up in the furs so warm,
Driving like mad over village and farm,
O'er the country drear, o'er the city towers,
Until you stopped at this house of ours?
Did you think 'twas a little girl like me
You were coming so fast thro' the snow to see?
Well, whatever way you happened here,
You are my pet and my treasure dear—
Such a Christmas present! O such a joy!
Better than any kind of a toy!
Something that eats and drinks and walks,
And looks so lovely and *almost* talks;
With a face so comical and wise,
And such a pair of bright brown eyes!
I'll tell you something: The other day
I heard papa to my mamma say
Very softly, "I really fear
Our baby may be quite spoiled, my dear,
We've made of our darling such a pet,
I think the little one may forget
There's any creature beneath the sun
Beside herself to waste thought upon."

I'm going to show him what I can do
For a dumb little helpless thing like you.
I'll not be selfish and slight you, dear;
Whenever I can I shall keep you near.

CELIA THAXTER.

SOME EDUCATED HORSES.

A NOD OF GREETING.

One of the most pleasing of modern English authors, Philip Gilbert Hamerton, who is an artist as well as writer, and who loves animals almost as he does art, says that it would be interesting for a man to live permanently in a large hall into which three or four horses, of a race already intelligent, should be allowed to go and come freely from the time they were born, just as dogs do in a family where they are pets, or something to that effect. They should have full liberty to poke their noses in their master's face, or lay their heads on his shoulder at meal-time, receiving their treat of lettuce or sugar or bread, only they must understand that they would be punished if they knocked off the vases or upset furniture, or did other mischief. He would like to see this tried, and see what would come of it; what intelligence a horse would develop, and what love.

The plan looks quixotic, does it not? But one thing you may be sure of; he might have worse associates. There are grades of intellect—we will call it intellect, for it comes very near, *so* near that we never can know just where the fine shading off begins between a horse's brain and that of a man; and there are warm, loving equine hearts. Many horses are superior to many men; nobler, more honorable, quicker-witted, more loyal, and a thousand times more companionable. Would you not rather, if you had to live on Robinson Crusoe's island, have an intelligent, sympathetic horse and a devoted bright dog than some people you know? One is inclined to favor Hamerton's notion after seeing the Bartholomew Educated Horses, who can do almost anything but speak.

BUCEPHALUS TAKES THE
HAT.

I am writing this for boys and girls who love animals, and for those elderly people who are fond of them too, including the lady whom I overheard saying that she had been nine times to see the remarkable exhibition. The young folks were enthusiastic patrons of that little theatre in Boston, where for more than a hundred afternoons and evenings the "Professor," as he was called, showed off his four-footed pupils. One forenoon he set apart for a free entertainment of as many poor children as the house would hold, who went under the charge of the truant officers and had an overwhelming good time.

There were sixteen of the animals, counting a donkey; grays, bays, chestnut-colored beauties, and one who looked buff in the gaslight. In recalling them, I cannot say that there was a white-footed one. What consequence about white feet, you ask! Perhaps you know that they make that of some account in the horse bazaars of the East. The Turks say "two white fore feet are lucky; one white fore and hind foot are unlucky;" and they have a rhyme that runs—

One white foot, buy a horse,
Two white feet, try a horse,
Three white feet, look well about him,
Four white feet, do without him.

THE CHAIR IS BROUGHT.

They were all named. There was a Chevalier, a Prince, and a Pope; a little pet, Miss Nellie, who looked as if she would be ready to drink tea out of your saucer and kiss you after her fashion; Mustang, an irrepressible and rude savage from the Rio Grande region; Brutus, Cæsar, and Draco; a Broncho beauty; a Sprite; a stately stepping Abdallah; Jim, who was a character; and a Bucephalus, after that storied steed who would suffer no one to ride but his master, the Great Alexander, but for him to mount, would kneel and wait.

It is perhaps needless and an insult to their intelligence for me to say that they all know their own names as well as you know yours. They know, too, their numbers when they are acting as soldiers formed in line waiting orders; the Professor passes along and checking them off with his forefinger numbers them, then falling back, calls out for certain ones to form into platoons, and they make no mistake. Their ears are alert, their senses sharp, their memory good. "Number Two," "Number Four," and so on, answer by advancing, as a soldier would respond to the roll-call.

They came around from the stable an hour before the performance and went up the stairs by which the audience went; and a crowd used to gather every afternoon and evening to see that remarkable and free feat.

PRINCE.

When the curtain rose there was to be seen a small stage carpeted ankle deep with saw-dust, where Professor Bartholomew purposed to have his horses act; first the part of a school, then of a court room, last a military drill and taking of a fort. They came in one after another, pretending, if that is not too strong a word, that they were on the way to school, and that was the playground; and there they played together, with such soft, graceful action, such caressing ways, and trippings as dainty as in "Pinafore," until at the ringing of a bell they came at once to order from their mixed-up, mazy pastime, and waited the arrival of their teacher, the Professor, who entered with a schoolmaster air, and gave the order.

"Bucephalus, take my hat, and bring me a chair!" as you might tell James or John to do the same, and with more promptness than they would have shown, Bucephalus came forward, took the hat between his teeth, carried it across the stage and placed it on a desk, and brought a chair.

SPRITE AS A MATHEMATICIAN.

The master, seating himself, began the business of the day, saying, "The school will now form two classes; the large scholars will go to the left, the small ones to the right;" and six magnificent creatures separated themselves from the group huddled together and went as they were bid, while Nellie, the mustang, and other little ones, filed off to the opposite side, and placed themselves in a row, with their heads turned away from the stage. And there they remained, generally minding their business, though sometimes one would get out of position, look around, or give his neighbor a nudge which brought out a reprimand: "Pope, what are you doing?" "Brutus, you need not look around to see what I am about!" "Sprite, you let Mustang alone!" "Mustang, keep in your place!"

He then called for some one to come forward and be monitor, and Prince volunteered, was sent to the desk for some papers, tried to raise the lid, and let it drop, pretending that he couldn't, but after being sharply asked what he was so careless for, did it, and then brought a handkerchief and made a great ado about wanting to have something done with it, which proved to be tying it around his leg. Meanwhile one of the horses behaved badly, whereupon the teacher said, "I see you are booked for a whipping," and the culprit came out in the floor, straightened himself, and received without wincing what seemed to be a severe whipping; but in reality it was all done with a soft cotton snapper, which made more sound than anything else.

ABDALLAH PACES.

Mustang was called upon to ring the bell, a good-sized dinner-bell, for the blackboard exercises by Sprite. He, too, made believe he couldn't, seized it the wrong way, dropped it, picked it up wrong end first, was scolded at, then took it by the handle, gave it a vigorous shake, and after letting it fall several times, set it on the table. Meanwhile a platform was brought in supporting a tall post, at the top of which, higher than a horse could reach, was a blackboard having chalked on it a sum which was not added up correctly. Sprite, being requested to wipe it out, took the sponge from the table, and planting her fore-feet on the platform, stretched her head up, and by desperate passes succeeded in wiping out a part of the figures, and started to leave, but seeing that some remained, went back and erased them.

One day she went through a process which showed conclusively that horses can reason. She dropped the sponge the first thing, and it fell down behind the platform out of her sight. She got down, and looked about in the saw-dust for it, the audience curiously watching to see what she would do next. She was evidently much perplexed. She knew perfectly well that her duty would not be fulfilled until she had rubbed the figures out, and the sponge was not to be found. Mr. Bartholomew said nothing, gave her no look or hint or sign to help her out of her predicament, but sat in his chair and waited. At last she deliberately stepped on the platform again, stretched her head up and wiped the figures out with her mouth, at which the audience applauded as if they would bring the roof down. That was something clearly not in the programme, but a bit of independent reasoning. Yet, having done so much, she knew that something was not right. About that sponge—what had become of it? It was her business to lay it on the table when she was through using it. She hesitated, looked this way and that, started to go, came back, dreadfully puzzled and uncertain, suddenly spied it, set her teeth in it, put it on the table, and went to her place, with a clear conscience, no doubt, and the people cheered more wildly than before.

A GAME OF LEAP-FROG.

This was to me one of the most interesting things I witnessed; and connecting it with some facts Mr. Bartholomew communicated, it was doubly so.

NELLIE ROLLS THE BARREL OVER THE "TETER."

He said that it was his practice not to interfere or help; the horse knew just what she was to do, and he preferred to wait and let her think it out for herself. The other horses all knew too if there was any failure or mistake, and the offender was closely watched by them, and in some way reproved by them if they could get the opportunity, and at times this little by-play became very amusing.

After this was most exquisite dancing by Bucephalus, and by Cæsar, whose steppings were in perfect rhythm to the music. Then the latter turned in a circle to the right or the left and walked around defining the figure eight, just as any one in the audience chose to request; and Abdallah came in with a string of bells around her, and paced, cantered, galloped, trotted, marched or walked as the word was given. The horses were generally expected to come to the footlights and bow to the audience at the close of any feat; occasionally one would forget to do this, and then some of his comrades would shoulder or buffet him, or Mr. Bartholomew would give a reminder, "That is not all, is it?" and back would come the delinquent, and bow and bow twenty times as fast as he could, as if there could not be enough of it. At the close of one scene all the horses came up to the front in a line, and leaning over the rope which was stretched there to keep them from coming down on the people's heads, would bow, and bow again, and it was a wonderfully pretty sight to see.

A game of leap frog was announced. "There are four of the horses that jump," said Mr. Bartholomew. They like this least of any of their feats, and those who can do it best are most timid. At first one horse is jumped over, then two, three, are packed closely together, and little Sprite clears them all at one flying leap, broad-backed and much taller than herself though they are. Those who do not want to try it beg off by a pretty pantomime, and Sprite is encouraged by her master, who pats her first and seems to be saying something in her ear. They like to get approval in the way of a caress, but beyond that they are in no way rewarded.

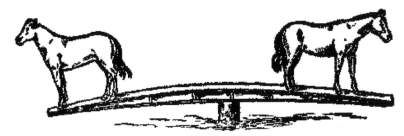

PRINCE AND POPE PLAY AT SEE-SAW.

Next Nellie rolled a barrel over a "teter plank" with her fore-feet, and Prince and Pope performed the difficult feat, and one which required mutual understanding and confidence, of see-sawing away up in air on the plank; first face to face, carefully balancing, and then the latter slowly turned on the space less than twenty inches wide, without disturbing the delicate poise. This he considers one of the most remarkable, because each horse must act with reference to the other, and the understanding between them must be so perfect that no fatal false movement can be made.

One of the grand tableaux represents a court scene with the donkey set up in a high place for judge, the jury passing around from mouth to mouth a placard labelled "Not Guilty," and the releasing of the prisoner from his chain. But the military drill exceeds all else by the brilliance of the display and the inspiring movements and martial air. Mr. Bartholomew in military uniform advancing like a general, disciplined twelve horses who came in at bugle call, with a crimson band about their bodies and other decorations, and went through evolutions, marchings, counter-marchings, in single file, by twos, in platoons, forming a hollow square with the precision of old soldiers. They liked it too, and were proud of themselves as they stepped to the music. The final act was a furious charge on a fort, the horses firing cannon, till in smoke and flame, to the sound of patriotic strains, the structure was demolished, the country's flag was saved, caught up by one horse, seized by another, waved, passed around, and amidst the excitement and confusion of a great victory, triumphant horses rushing about, the curtain fell.

THE GREAT COURT SCENE.

It was from first to last a wonderful exhibition of horse intelligence.

Trained horses, that is, trained for circus feats at given signals, are no novelty. Away back in the reign of one of the Stuarts, a horse named Morocco was exhibited in England, though his tricks were only as the alphabet to what is done now. And long before Rarey's day, there was here and there a man who had a sort of magnetic influence, and could tame a vicious horse whom nobody else dared go near. When George the Fourth was Prince of Wales, he had a valuable Egyptian horse who would throw, they said, the best rider in the world. Even if a man could succeed in getting on his back, it was not an instant he could stay there. But there came to England on a visit a distinguished Eastern bey, with his mamelukes, who, hearing of the matter which was the talk of the town, declared that the animal should be ridden. Accordingly many royal personages and noblemen met the Orientals at the riding house of the Prince, in Pall Mall, a mameluke's saddle was put on the vicious creature, who was led in, looking in a white heat of fury, wicked, with danger in his eyes, when, behold, the bey's chief officer sprung on his back and rode for half an hour as easily as a lady would amble on the most spiritless pony that ever was bridled.

STRETCHING HIMSELF.

Some men have a tact, a way with animals, and can do anything with them. It is a born gift, a rare one, and a precious one. There was a certain tamer of lions and tigers, Henri Marten by name, who lately died at the age of ninety, who tamed by his personal influence alone. It was said of him in France, that at the head of an army he "might have been a Bonaparte. Chance has made a man of genius a director of a menagerie."

Professor Bartholomew was ready to talk about his way, but a part of it is the man himself. He could not make known to another what is the most essential requisite. He, too, brought genius to his work; besides that, a certain indefinable mastership which animals recognize, love for them, and a vast amount of perseverance and patient waiting. It is a thing that is not done in a day.

He was fond of horses from a boy, and began early to educate one, having a remarkable faculty for handling them; so that now, after thirty years of it, there is not much about the equine nature that he does not understand. He trained a company of Bronchos, which were afterwards sold; and since then he has gradually got together the fifteen he now exhibits, and he has others in process of training. He took these when they were young, two or three years old; and not one of them, except Jim, who has a bit of outside history, has ever been used in any other way. They know nothing about carriages or carts, harness or saddle; they have escaped the cruel curb-bits, the check reins and blinders of our civilization. Fortunate in that respect. And they never have had a shoe on their feet. Their feet are perfect, firm and sound, strong and healthy and elastic; natural, like those of the Indians, who run barefoot, who go over the rough places of the wilds as easily as these horses can run up the stairs or over the cobble stones of the pavement if they were turned loose in the street.

MILITARY DRILL.

It was a pleasure to know of their life-long exemption from all such restraints. That accounted in great measure for their beautiful freedom of motion, for that wondrous grace and charm. Did you ever think what a complexity of muscles, bones, joints, tendons and other arrangements, enter into the formation of the knees, hoofs, legs of a horse; what a piece of mechanism the strong, supple creature is?

These have never had their spirits broken; have never been scolded at or struck except when a whip was necessary as a rod sometimes is for a child. The hostlers who take care of them are not allowed to speak roughly. "Be low-spoken to them," the master says. In the years when he was educating them he groomed and cared for them himself, with no other help except that of his two little sons. No one else was allowed to meddle with them; and, necessarily, they were kept separate from other horses. Now, wherever they are exhibiting, he always goes out the first thing in the morning to see them. He passes from one to another, and they are all expecting the little love pats and slaps on their glossy sides, the caressings and fondlings and pleasant greetings of "Chevalier, how are you, old fellow?" "Abdallah, my beauty," and, "Nellie, my pet!" Some are jealous, Abdallah tremendously so, and if he does not at once notice her, she lays her ears back, shows temper, and crowds up to him, determined that no other shall have precedence.

A PRETTY TABLEAU.

They are not "thorough-breds." Those, he said, were for racers or travellers; yet of fine breeds, some choice blood horses, some mixed, one a mustang, who at first did not know anything that was wanted of him.

"Why," said he, "at first some of them would go up like pop corn, higher than my head. But I never once have been injured by one of them except perhaps an accidental stepping on my foot. They never kick; they don't know how to kick. You can go behind them as well as before, and anywhere."

In buying he chose only those whose looks showed that they were intelligent. "But how did he know, by what signs?" queried an all-absorbed "Dumb Animals" woman.

"Oh, dear," he said, "why, every way; the eyes, the ears, the whole face, the expression, everything. No two horses' faces look alike. Just as it is with a flock of sheep. A stranger would say, 'Why, they are all sheep, and all alike, and that is all there is to it;' but the owner knows better; he knows every face in the flock. He says, 'this is Jenny, and that is Dolly, there is Jim, and here's Nancy.' Oh, land, yes! they are no more alike than human beings are, disposition or anything. Some have to be ordered, and some coaxed and flattered. Yes, flattered. Now if two men come and want to work for me, I can tell as soon as I cast my eyes on them. I say to one, 'Go and do such a thing;' but if I said it to the other, he'd answer 'I won't; I'm not going to be ordered about by any man.' Horses are just like that. A horse can read you. If you get mad, he will. If you abuse him, he will do the same by you, or try to. You must control yourself, if you would control a horse."

They must be of superior grade, "for it's of no use to spend one's time on a dull one. It does not pay to teach idiots where you want brilliant results, though all well enough for a certain purpose."

Some of these he had been five years in educating to do what we saw. Some he had taught to do their special part in one year, some in two. The first thing he did was to give the horse opportunity and time to get well acquainted with him; in his words, "to become friends. Let him see that you are his friend, that you are not going to whip him. You meet him cordially. You are glad to see him and be with him, and pretty soon he knows it and likes to be with you. And so you establish comradeship, you understand each other. Caress him softly. Don't make a dash at him. Say pleasant things to him. Be gentle; but at the same time you must be *master*." That is a good basis. And then he teaches one thing at a time, a simple thing, and waits a good while before he brings forward another; does not perplex or puzzle the pupil by anything else till that is learned, and some of the first words are "come," "stand," "remain."

What a horse has once learned he never or seldom forgets. Mr. Bartholomew thinks it is not as has sometimes been said, because a horse has a memory stronger than a man, "but because he has fewer things to learn. A man sees a million things. A horse's mind cannot accommodate what a man's can, so those things he knows have a better chance. Those few things he fixes. His memory fastens on them. I once had a pony I had trained, which was afterwards gone from me three years. At the end of that time I was in California exhibiting, and saw a boy on the pony. I tried to buy him, but the boy who had owned him all that time, refused to part with him; however, I offered such a price that I got him, and that same evening I took him into the tent and thought I would see what he remembered. He went through all his old tricks (besides a few I had myself forgotten) except one. He could not manage walking on his hind feet the distance he used to. Another time I had a trained horse stolen from me by the Indians, and he was off in the wilds with them a year and a half. One day, in a little village—that was in California too—I saw him and knew him, and the horse knew me. I went up to the Indian who had him and said, 'That is my horse, and I can prove it.' Out there a stolen horse, no matter how many times he has changed hands, is given up, if the owner can prove it. The Indian said, 'If you can, you shall have him, but you won't do it.' I said, 'I will try him in four things; I will ask him to trot three times around a circle, to lie down, to sit up, and to bring me my handkerchief. If he is my horse, he will do it.' The Indian said, 'You shall have him if he does, but he won't!' By this time a crowd had got together. We put the horse in an enclosure, he did as he was told, and I had him back."

Mr. Bartholomew said, "My motto in educating them is, 'Make haste slowly;' I never require too much, and I never ask a horse to do what he *can't* do. That is of no use. A horse *can't* learn what horses are not capable of learning; and he can't do a thing until he understands what you mean, and how you want it done. What good would it do for me to ask a man a question in French if he did not know a word of the language? I get him used to the word, and show him what I want. If it is to climb up somewhere, I gently put his foot up and have him keep it there until I am ready to have it come down, and then I take it down myself. I never let the horse do it. The same with other things, showing him how, and by words. They know a great number of words. My horses are not influenced by signs or motions when they are on the stage. They use their intelligence and memory, and they associate ideas and are required to obey. They learn a great deal by observing one another. One watches and learns by seeing the others. I taught one horse to kneel, by first bending his knee myself, and putting him into position. After he had learned, I took another in who kept watch all the time, and learned partly by imitation. They are social creatures; they love each other's company."

Most of these horses have been together now for several years, and are fond of one another. They appear to keep the run of the whole performance, and listen and notice like children in a school when one or more of their number goes out to recite. It was extremely interesting to observe them when the leap-frog game was going on. Owing to the smallness of the stage, it was difficult for the horse who was to make the jump to get under headway, and several times poor Sprite, or whichever it was, would turn abruptly to make another start, upon which every horse on her side would dart out for a chance at giving her a nip as she went by. They all seemed throughout the entire exhibition to feel a sort of responsibility, or at least a pride in it, as if "this is *our* school. See how well Bucephalus minds, or how badly Brutus behaves! This is *our* regiment. Don't we march well? How fine and grand, how gallant and gay we are!" And the wonder of it all is, not so much what any one horse can do, or the sense of humor they show, or the great number of words they understand, but the mental processes and nice calculation they show in the feats where they are associated in complex ways, which require that each must act his part independently and mind nothing about it if another happens to make a mistake.

VICTORY.

To obtain any adequate representation of these horses while performing, it was necessary that it be done by process called instantaneous photographing. You are aware that birds and insects are taken by means of an instrument named the "photographic revolver," which is aimed at them. Recently an American, Mr. Muybridge, has been able to photograph horses while galloping or trotting, by his "battery of cameras," and a book on "the Horse in Motion" has for its subject this instantaneous catching a likeness as applied to animals. But how could any process, however swift, or ingenious, or admirable, do full justice to the grace and spirit, the all-alive attitudes and varieties of posture, the dalliance and charm, the freedom in action?

THE STORMING OF THE FORT.

Professor Bartholomew gave his performances the name of "The Equine Paradox." He now has his beautiful animals in delightful summer quarters at Newport, where they are counted among the "notable guests." He has the Opera House there for his training school for three months, preparing new ones for next winter's exhibition, and keeping the old ones in practice. It is pleasant to know that he cares so faithfully for their health as to give them a home through the warm weather in that cool retreat by the sea.

QUESTIONS.

Can you put the spider's web back in its place, that once has been swept away?

Can you put the apple again on the bough, which fell at our feet to-day?

Can you put the lily-cup back on the stem, and cause it to live and grow?

Can you mend the butterfly's broken wing, that you crushed with a hasty blow?

Can you put the bloom again on the grape, or the grape again on the vine?

Can you put the dewdrops back on the flowers, and make them sparkle and shine?

Can you put the petals back on the rose? If you could, would it smell as sweet?

Can you put the flour again in the husk, and show me the ripened wheat?

Can you put the kernel back in the nut, or the broken egg in its shell?

Can you put the honey back in the comb, and cover with wax each cell?

Can you put the perfume back in the vase, when once it has sped away?

Can you put the corn-silk back on the corn, or the down on the catkins—say?

You think that my questions are trifling, dear? Let me ask you another one:

Can a hasty word ever be unsaid, or a deed unkind, undone?

KATE LAWRENCE.

THE BRAVEST BOY IN TOWN.

He lived in the Cumberland Valley,
   And his name was Jamie Brown;
But it changed one day, so the neighbors say,
   To the "Bravest Boy in Town."

'Twas the time when the Southern soldiers,
   Under Early's mad command,
O'er the border made their dashing raid
   From the north of Maryland.

And Chambersburg unransomed
   In smouldering ruins slept,
While up the vale, like a fiery gale,
   The Rebel raiders swept.

And a squad of gray-clad horsemen
   Came thundering o'er the bridge,
Where peaceful cows in the meadows browse,
   At the feet of the great Blue Ridge;

And on till they reached the village,
   That fair in the valley lay,
Defenseless then, for its loyal men,
   At the front, were far away.

"Pillage and spoil and plunder!"
   This was the fearful word
That the Widow Brown, in gazing down
   From her latticed window, heard.

'Neath the boughs of the sheltering oak-tree,
   The leader bared his head,

As left and right, until out of sight,
    His dusty gray-coats sped.

Then he called: "Halloo! within there!"
    A gentle, fair-haired dame
Across the floor to the open door
    In gracious answer came.

"Here! stable my horse, you woman!"—
    The soldier's tones were rude—
"Then bestir yourself and from yonder shelf
    Set out your store of food!"

For her guest she spread the table;
    She motioned him to his place
With a gesture proud; then the widow bowed,
    And gently—asked a grace.

"If thine enemy hunger, feed him!
    I obey, dear Christ!" she said;
A creeping blush, with its scarlet flush,
    O'er the face of the soldier spread.

He rose: "You have said it, madam!
    Standing within your doors
Is the Rebel foe; but as forth they go
    They shall trouble not you nor yours!"

Alas, for the word of the leader!
    Alas, for the soldier's vow!
When the captain's men rode down the glen,
    They carried the widow's cow.

It was then the fearless Jamie
    Sprang up with flashing eyes,
And in spite of tears and his mother's fears,
    On the gray mare, off he flies.

Like a wild young Tam O'Shanter

He plunged with piercing whoop,
O'er field and brook till he overtook
    The straggling Rebel troop.

Laden with spoil and plunder,
    And laughing and shouting still,
As with cattle and sheep they lazily creep
    Through the dust o'er the winding hill.

"Oh! the coward crowd!" cried Jamie;
    "There's Brindle! I'll teach them now!"
And with headlong stride, at the captain's side,
    He called for his mother's cow.

"Who are *you*, and who is your mother?—
    I promised she should not miss?—
Well! upon my word, have I never heard
    Of assurance like to this!"

"Is your word the word of a soldier?"—
    And the young lad faced his foes,
As a jeering laugh, in anger half
    And half in sport, arose.

But the captain drew his sabre,
    And spoke, with lowering brow:
"Fall back into line! The joke is mine!
    Surrender the widow's cow!"

And a capital joke they thought it,
    That a barefoot lad of ten
Should demand his due—and get it too—
    In the face of forty men.

And the rollicking Rebel raiders
    Forgot themselves somehow,
And three cheers brave for the hero gave,
    And three for the brindle cow.

He lived in the Cumberland Valley,
    And his name *was* Jamie Brown;
But it changed that day, so the neighbors say,
    To the "Bravest Boy in Town."

MRS. EMILY HUNTINGTON NASON.

THE WOLF AND THE GOSLINGS.

An old gray goose walked forth with pride,
With goslings seven at her side;
A lovely yellowish-green they were,
    And very dear to her.

She led them to the river's brink
To paddle their feet awhile and drink,
And there she heard a tale that made
    Her very soul afraid.

A neighbor gabbled the story out,
How a wolf was known to be thereabout—
A great wolf whom nothing could please
    As well as little geese.

So, when, as usual, to the wood
She went next day in search of food,
She warned them over and over, before
    She turned to shut the door:

"My little ones, if you hear a knock
At the door, be sure and not unlock,
For the wolf will eat you, if he gets in,
　　Feathers and bones and skin.

"You will know him by his voice so hoarse,
By his paws so hairy and black and coarse."
And the goslings piped up, clear and shrill,
　　"We'll take great care, we will."

The mother thought them wise and went
To the far-off forest quite content;
But she was scarcely away, before
　　There came a rap at the door.

"Open, open, my children dear,"
A gruff voice cried: "your mother is here."
But the young ones answered, "No, no, no,
　　Her voice is sweet and low;

"And you are the wolf—so go away,
You can't get in, if you try all day."
He laughed to himself to hear them talk,
   And wished he had some chalk,

To smooth his voice to a tone like geese;
So he went to the merchant's and bought a piece,
And hurried back, and rapped once more.
   "Open, open the door,

"I am your mother, dears," he said.
But up on the window ledge he laid,
In a careless way, his great black paw,
   And this the goslings saw.

"No, no," they called, "that will not do,
Our mother has not black hands like you;
For you are the wolf, so go away,
   You can't get in to-day."

The baffled wolf to the old mill ran,
And whined to the busy miller man:
"I love to hear the sound of the wheel
   And to smell the corn and meal."

The miller was pleased, and said "All right;
Would you like your cap and jacket white?"
At that he opened a flour bin
   And playfully dipped him in.

He floundered and sneezed a while, then, lo,
He crept out white as a wolf of snow.
"If chalk and flour can make me sweet,"
   He said, "then I'm complete."

For the third time back to the house he went,
And looked and spoke so different,
That when he rapped, and "Open!" cried,
   The little ones replied,

"If you show us nice clean feet, we will."
And straightway, there on the window-sill
His paws were laid, with dusty meal
   Powdered from toe to heel.

Yes, they were white! So they let him in,
And he gobbled them all up, feathers and skin!
Gobbled the whole, as if 'twere fun,
    Except the littlest one.

An old clock stood there, tick, tick, tick,
And into that he had hopped so quick
The wolf saw nothing, and fancied even
    He'd eaten all the seven.

But six were enough to satisfy;
So out he strolled on the grass to lie.
And when the gray goose presently
    Came home—what did she see?

Alas, the house door open wide,
But no little yellow flock inside;
The beds and pillows thrown about;
    The fire all gone out;

The chairs and tables overset;
The wash-tub spilled, and the floor all wet;
And here and there in cinders black,
    The great wolf's ugly track.

She called out tenderly every name,
But never a voice in answer came,
Till a little frightened, broad-billed face
    Peered out of the clock-case.

This gosling told his tale with grief,
And the gray goose sobbed in her handkerchief,
And sighed—"Ah, well, we will have to go
    And let the neighbors know."

So down they went to the river's brim,
Where their feathered friends were wont to swim,
And there on the turf so green and deep
    The old wolf lay asleep.

He had a grizzly, savage look,
And he snored till the boughs above him shook.
They tiptoed round him—drew quite near,
    Yet still he did not hear.

Then, as the mother gazed, to her
It seemed she could see his gaunt side stir—

Stir and squirm, as if under the skin
  Were something alive within!

"Go back to the house, quick, dear," she said,
"And fetch me scissors and needle and thread.
I'll open his ugly hairy hide,
  And see what is inside."

She snipped with the scissors a criss-cross slit,
And well rewarded she was for it,
For there were her goslings—six together—
  With scarcely a rumpled feather.

The wolf had eaten so greedily,
He had swallowed them all alive you see,
So, one by one, they scrambled out,

And danced and skipped about.

Then the gray goose got six heavy stones,
And placed them in between the bones;
She sewed him deftly, with needle and thread,
　　And then with her goslings fled.

The wolf slept long and hard and late,
And woke so thirsty he scarce could wait.
So he crept along to the river's brink
　　To get a good cool drink.

But the stones inside began to shake,
And make his old ribs crack and ache;
And the gladsome flock, as they sped away,
　　Could hear him groan, and say:—

"What's this rumbling and tumbling?
What's this rattling like bones?
I thought I'd eaten six small geese,
　　But they've turned out only stones."

He bent his neck to lap—instead,
He tumbled in, heels over head;
And so heavy he was, as he went down
　　He could not help but drown!

And after that, in thankful pride,
With goslings seven at her side,
The gray goose came to the river's brink
　　Each day to swim and drink.

AMANDA B. HARRIS.

THE BISHOP'S VISIT.

Tell you about it? Of course I will!
I thought 'twould be dreadful to have him come,
For mamma said I must be quiet and still,
And she put away my whistle and drum.—

And made me unharness the parlor chairs,
And packed my cannon and all the rest
Of my noisiest playthings off up-stairs,
On account of this very distinguished guest.

Then every room was turned upside down,
And all the carpets hung out to blow;
For when the Bishop is coming to town
The house must be in order, you know.

So out in the kitchen I made my lair,
And started a game of hide-and-seek;
But Bridget refused to have me there,
For the Bishop was coming—to stay a week—

And she must have cookies and cakes and pies,
And fill every closet and platter and pan,
Till I thought this Bishop, so great and wise,
Must be an awfully hungry man.

Well! at last he came; and I do declare,
Dear grandpapa, he looked just like you,
With his gentle voice and his silvery hair,
And eyes with a smile a-shining through.

And whenever he read or talked or prayed,
I understood every single word;
And I wasn't the leastest bit afraid,
Though I never once spoke or stirred;

Till, all of a sudden, he laughed right out
To see me sit quietly listening so;
And began to tell us stories about
Some queer little fellows in Mexico.

And all about Egypt and Spain—and then
He *wasn't* disturbed by a little noise,
And said that the greatest and best of men
Once were rollicking, healthy boys.

And he thinks it is no matter at all
If a little boy runs and jumps and climbs;
And mamma should be willing to let me crawl
Through the bannister-rails in the hall sometimes.

And Bridget, sir, made a great mistake,
In stirring up such a bother, you see,
For the Bishop—he didn't care for cake,
And really liked to play games with me.

But though he's so honored in word and act—
(Stoop down, this is a secret now)—
He couldn't spell Boston! That's a fact!
But whispered to me to tell him how.

MRS. EMMA HUNTINGTON NASON.

THE FIRST STEP.

To-night as the tender gloaming
　　Was sinking in evening's gloom,
And only the glow of the firelight
　　Brightened the dark'ning room,
I laughed with the gay heart-gladness
　　That only to mothers is known,
For the beautiful brown-eyed baby
　　Took his first step alone!

BABY'S FIRST STEP.

Hurriedly running to meet him
  Came trooping the household band,
Joyous, loving and eager
  To reach him a helping hand,
To watch him with silent rapture,
  To cheer him with happy noise,
My one little fair-faced daughter
  And four brown romping boys.

Leaving the sheltering arms
  That fain would bid him rest
Close to the love and the longing,
  Near to the mother's breast;
Wild with laughter and daring,
  Looking askance at me,
He stumbled across through the shadows
  To rest at his father's knee.

Baby, my dainty darling,
  Stepping so brave and bright
With flutter of lace and ribbon
  Out of my arms to-night,
Helped in thy pretty ambition
  With tenderness blessed to see,
Sheltered, upheld, and protected—
  How will the last step be?

See, we are all beside you
  Urging and beckoning on,
Watching lest aught betide you
  Till the safe near goal is won,
Guiding the faltering footsteps
  That tremble and fear to fall—
How will it be, my darling,
  With the last sad step of all?

Nay! Shall I dare to question,
  Knowing that One more fond
Than all our tenderest loving

Will guide the weak feet beyond!
And knowing beside, my dearest,
    That whenever the summons, 'twill be
But a stumbling step through the shadows,
    Then rest—at the Father's knee!

M.E.B.

BINGEN ON THE RHINE.

A Soldier of the Legion lay dying in Algiers,
There was lack of woman's nursing, there was dearth of woman's tears;
But a comrade stood beside him while his life-blood ebbed away,
And bent with pitying glances to hear what he might say.
The dying soldier faltered, as he took that comrade's hand,
And he said, "I never more shall see my own, my native land;
Take a message, and a token to some distant friends of mine,
For I was born at Bingen, at Bingen on the Rhine.

"Tell my brothers and companions when they meet and crowd around
To hear my mournful story, in the pleasant vineyard ground,
That we fought the battle bravely, and when the day was done,
Full many a corse lay ghastly pale beneath the setting sun;
And, 'mid the dead and dying, were some grown old in wars,
The death-wound on their gallant breasts, the last of many scars;
And some were young, and suddenly beheld life's morn decline,
And one had come from Bingen, fair Bingen on the Rhine.

"Tell my mother that her other son shall comfort her old age;
For I was still a truant bird, that thought his home a cage.
For my father was a soldier, and even as a child
My heart leaped forth to hear him tell of struggles fierce and wild;
And when he died and left us to divide his scanty hoard
I let them take whate'er they would, but I kept my father's sword;
And with boyish love I hung it where the bright light used to shine
On the cottage wall at Bingen, calm Bingen on the Rhine.

"Tell my sister not to weep for me, and sob with drooping head,
When the troops come marching home again with glad and gallant tread,
But to look upon them proudly, with a calm and steadfast eye,
For her brother was a soldier, too, and not afraid to die;
And if a comrade seek her love, I ask her in my name,

To listen to him kindly, without regret or shame,
And to hang the old sword in its place, my father's sword and mine;
For the honor of old Bingen, dear Bingen on the Rhine.

"There's another, not a sister, in the happy days gone by,
You'd have known her by the merriment that sparkled in her eye;
Too innocent for coquetry, too fond for idle scorning,
O, friend! I fear the lightest heart makes sometimes heaviest mourning.
Tell her the last night of my life (for ere the moon be risen
My body will be out of pain, my soul be out of prison),
I dreamed I stood with her, and saw the yellow sunlight shine,
On the vine-clad hills of Bingen, fair Bingen on the Rhine.

"I saw the blue Rhine sweep along; I heard, or seemed to hear,
The German songs we used to sing in chorus sweet and clear;
And down the pleasant river and up the slanting hill,
The echoing chorus sounded, through the evening calm and still;
And her glad blue eyes were on me, as we passed, with friendly talk
Down many a path beloved of yore, and well remembered walk,
And her little hand lay lightly, confidingly, in mine,
But we'll meet no more at Bingen, loved Bingen on the Rhine."

His trembling voice grew faint and hoarse, his grasp was childish weak,
His eyes put on a dying look, he sighed, and ceased to speak;
His comrade bent to lift him, but the spark of life had fled—
The soldier of the Legion in a foreign land is dead;
And the soft moon rose up slowly, and calmly she looked down
On the red sand of the battle-field with bloody corses strewn;
Yet calmly on that dreadful scene her pale light seemed to shine,
As it shone on distant Bingen, fair Bingen on the Rhine.

CAROLINE E.S. NORTON.

OSITO.

On the lofty mountain that faced the captain's cabin the frost had already made an insidious approach, and the slender thickets of quaking ash that marked the course of each tiny torrent, now stood out in resplendent hues and shone afar off like gay ribbons running through the dark-green pines. Gorgeously, too, with scarlet, crimson and gold, gleamed the lower spurs, where the oak-brush grew in dense masses and bore beneath a blaze of color, a goodly harvest of acorns, now ripe and loosened in their cups.

It was where one of these spurs joined the parent mountain, where the oak-brush grew thickest, and, as a consequence, the acorns were most abundant, that the captain, well versed in wood-craft mysteries, had built his bear trap. For two days he had been engaged upon it, and now, as the evening drew on, he sat contemplating it with satisfaction, as a work finished and perfected.

From his station there, on the breast of the lofty mountain, the captain could scan many an acre of sombre pine forest with pleasant little parks interspersed, and here and there long slopes brown with bunch grass. He was the lord of this wild domain. And yet his sway there was not undisputed. Behind an intervening spur to the westward ran an old Indian trail long traveled by the Southern Utes in their migrations north for trading and hunting purposes. And even now, a light smoke wafted upward on the evening air, told of a band encamped on the trail on their homeward journey to the Southwest.

The captain needed not this visual token of their proximity. He had been aware of it for several days. Their calls at his cabin in the lonely little park below had been frequent, and they had been specially solicitous of his coffee, his sugar, his biscuit and other delicacies, insomuch that once or twice during his absence these ingenuous children of Nature had with primitive simplicity, entered his cabin and helped themselves without leave or stint.

However, as he knew their stay would be short, the captain bore these neighborly attentions with mild forbearance. It was guests more graceless than these who had roused his wrath.

From their secret haunts far back towards the Snowy Range the bears had come down to feast upon the ripened acorns, and so doing, had scented the captain's bacon and sugar afar off and had prowled by night about the cabin. Nay, more, three days before, the captain, having gone hurriedly away and left the door loosely fastened, upon his return had found all in confusion. Many of his eatables had vanished, his flour sack was ripped open, and, unkindest cut of all, his beloved books lay scattered about. At the first indignant glance the captain had cried out, "Utes again!" But on looking around he saw a tell-tale trail left by floury bear paws.

Hence this bear trap.

It was but a strong log pen floored with rough-hewn slabs and fitted with a ponderous movable lid made of other slabs pinned on stout cross pieces. But, satisfied with his handiwork, the captain now arose, and, prying up one end of the lid with a lever, set the trigger and baited it with a huge piece of bacon. He then piled a great quantity of rock upon the already heavy lid to further guard against the escape of any bear so unfortunate as to enter, and shouldering his axe and rifle walked homewards.

Whatever vengeful visions of captive bears he was indulging in were, however, wholly dispelled as he drew near the cabin. Before the door stood the Ute chief accompanied by two squaws. "How!" said the chieftain, with a conciliatory smile, laying one hand on his breast of bronze and extending the other as the captain approached.

"How!" returned the captain bluffly, disdaining the hand with a recollection of sundry petty thefts.

"Has the great captain seen a pappoose about his wigwam?" asked the chief, nowise abashed, in Spanish—a language which many of the Southern Utes speak as fluently as their own.

The great captain had expected a request for a biscuit; he, therefore, was naturally surprised at being asked for a baby. With an effort he mustered together his Spanish phrases and managed to reply that he had seen no pappoose.

"Me pappoose lost," said one of the squaws brokenly. And there was so much distress in her voice that the captain, forgetting instantly all about the slight depredations of his dusky neighbors, volunteered to aid them in their search for the missing child.

All that night, for it was by this time nearly dark, the hills flared with pine torches and resounded with the shrill cries of the squaws, the whoops of the warriors, the shouts of the captain; but the search was fruitless.

This adventure drove the bear-trap from its builder's mind, and it was two days before it occurred to him to go there in quest of captive bears.

Coming in view of it he immediately saw the lid was down. Hastily he approached, bent over, and peeped in. And certainly, in the whole of his adventurous life the captain was never more taken by surprise; for there, crouched in one corner, was that precious Indian infant.

Yes, true it was, that all those massive timbers, all that ponderous mass of rock, had only availed to capture one very small Ute pappoose. At the thought of it, the builder of the trap was astounded. He laughed aloud at the absurdity. In silence he threw off the rock and lid and seated himself on the edge of the open trap. Captor and captive then gazed at each other with gravity. The errant infant's attire consisted of a calico shirt of gaudy hues, a pair of little moccasins, much frayed, and a red flannel string. This last was tied about his straggling hair, which fell over his forehead like the shaggy mane of a *bronco* colt and veiled, but could not obscure, the brightness of his black eyes.

He did not cry; in fact, this small stoic never even whimpered, but he held the bacon, or what remained of it, clasped tightly to his breast and gazed at his captor in silence. Glancing at the bacon, the captain saw it all. Hunger had induced this wee wanderer to enter the trap, and in detaching the bait, he had sprung the trigger and was caught.

"What are you called, little one?" asked the captain at length, in a reassuring voice, speaking Spanish very slowly and distinctly.

"Osito," replied the wanderer in a small piping voice, but with the dignity of a warrior.

"Little Bear!" the captain repeated, and burst into a hearty laugh, immediately checked, however by the thought that now he had caught him, what was he to do with him? The first thing, evidently, was to feed him.

So he conducted him to the cabin and there, observing the celerity with which the lumps of sugar vanished, he saw at once that Little Bear was most aptly named. Then, sometimes leading, and sometimes carrying him, for Osito was very small, he set out for the Ute encampment.

Their approach was the signal for a mighty shout. Warriors, squaws and the younger confrères of Osito, crowded about him. A few words from the captain explained all, and Osito himself, clinging to his mother, was borne away in triumph—the hero of the hour. Yet, no—the captain was that, I believe. For as he stood in their midst with a very pleased look on his sunburnt face, the chief quieting the hubbub with a wave of his hand, advanced and stood before him. "The great captain has a good heart," he said in tones of conviction. "What can his Ute friends do to show their gratitude?"

"Nothing," said the captain, looking more pleased than ever.

"The captain has been troubled by the bears. Would it please him if they were all driven back to their dens in the great mountains towards the setting sun?"

"It would," said the captain; "can it be done?"

"It can. It shall," said the chief with emphasis. "To-morrow let the *captain* keep his eyes open, and as the sun sinks behind the mountain tops he shall see the bears follow also."

The chief kept his word. The next day the uproar on the hills was terrific. Frightened out of their wits, the bears forsook the acorn field and fled ingloriously to their secret haunts in the mountains to the westward.

"WHAT ARE YOU CALLED, LITTLE ONE?" ASKED THE CAPTAIN.

In joy thereof the captain gave a great farewell feast to his red allies. It was spread under the pines in front of his cabin, and every delicacy of the season was there, from bear steaks to beaver tails. The banquet was drawing to a close, and complimentary speeches 'twixt host and guests were in order, when a procession of the squaws was seen approaching from the encampment. They drew near and headed for the captain in solemn silence. As they passed, each laid some gift at his feet—fringed leggings; beaded moccasins, bear skins, coyote skins, beaver pelts and soft robes of the mountain lion's hide—until the pile reached to the captain's shoulders. Last of all came Osito's mother and crowned the heap with a beautiful little brown bear skin. It was fancifully adorned with blue ribbons, and in the center of the tanned side there were drawn, in red pigment, the outlines of a very stolid and stoical-looking pappoose.

F.L. STEALEY.

THE LITTLE LION-CHARMER.

Outside the little village of Katrine,
  Just where the country ventures into town,
A circus pitched its tents, and on the green
  The canvas pyramids were fastened down.

The night was clear. The moon was climbing higher.
  The show was over; crowds were coming out,
When, through the surging mass, the cry of "fire!"
  Rose from a murmur to a wild, hoarse shout.

"Fire! fire!" The crackling flames ran up the tent,
  The shrieks of frightened women filled the air,
The cries of prisoned beasts weird horror lent
  To the wild scene of uproar and despair.

A lion's roar high over all the cries!
  There is a crash—out into the night
The tawny creature leaps with glowing eyes,
  Then stands defiant in the fierce red light.

"The lion's loose! The lion! Fly for your lives!"
  But deathlike silence falls upon them all,
So paralyzed with fear that no one strives
  To make escape, to move, to call!

"A weapon! Shoot him!" comes from far outside;
  The shout wakes men again to conscious life;
But as the aim is taken, the ranks divide
  To make a passage for the keeper's wife.

Alone she came, a woman tall and fair,
  And hurried on, and near the lion stood;

"Oh, do not fire!" she cried; "let no one dare
  To shoot my lion—he is tame and good.

"My son? my son?" she called; and to her ran
  A little child, that scarce had seen nine years.
"Play! play!" she said. Quickly the boy began.
  His little flute was heard by awe-struck ears.

"Fetch me a cage," she cried. The men obeyed.
  "Now go, my son, and bring the lion here."
Slowly the child advanced, and piped, and played,
  While men and women held their breaths in fear.

Sweetly he played, as though no horrid fate
  Could ever harm his sunny little head.
He never paused, nor seemed to hesitate,
  But went to do the thing his mother said.

The lion hearkened to the sweet clear sound;
  The anger vanished from his threatening eyes;
All motionless he crouched upon the ground
  And listened to the silver melodies.

The boy thus reached his side. The beast stirred not.
    The child then backward walked, and played again,
Till, moving softly, slowly from the spot,
    The lion followed the familiar strain.

The cage is waiting—wide its opened door—
    And toward it, cautiously, the child retreats.
But see! The lion, restless grown once more,
    Is lashing with his tail in angry beats.

The boy, advancing, plays again the lay.
    Again the beast, remembering the refrain,
Follows him on, until in this dread way
    The cage is reached, and in it go the twain.

At once the boy springs out, the door makes fast,
    Then leaps with joy to reach his mother's side;
Her praise alone, of all that crowd so vast,
    Has power to thrill his little heart with pride.

HARRIET S. FLEMING.

THE BOY TO THE SCHOOLMASTER.

You've quizzed me often and puzzled me long,
   You've asked me to cipher and spell,
You've called me a dunce if I answered wrong,
   Or a dolt if I failed to tell
Just when to say *lie* and when to say *lay*,
   Or what nine sevens may make,
Or the longitude of Kamschatka Bay,
   Or the I-forget-what's-its-name Lake,
So I think it's about *my* turn, I do,
To ask a question or so of you.

The schoolmaster grim, he opened his eyes,
But said not a word for sheer surprise.

Can you tell what "phen-dubs" means? I can.
   Can you say all off by heart
The "onery twoery ickery ann,"
   Or tell "alleys" and "commons" apart?
Can *you* fling a top, I would like to know,
   Till it hums like a bumble-bee?
Can you make a kite yourself that will go
   'Most as high as the eye can see,
Till it sails and soars like a hawk on the wing,
And the little birds come and light on its string?

The schoolmaster looked oh! very demure,
But his mouth was twitching, I'm almost sure.

Can you tell where the nest of the oriole swings,
   Or the color its eggs may be?
Do you know the time when the squirrel brings
   Its young from their nest in the tree?

Can you tell when the chestnuts are ready to drop
    Or where the best hazel-nuts grow?
Can you climb a high tree to the very tip-top,
    Then gaze without trembling below?
Can you swim and dive, can you jump and run,
Or do anything else we boys call fun?

The master's voice trembled as he replied:
"You are right, my lad, I'm the dunce," he sighed.

E.J. WHEELER.

WON'T TAKE A BAFF.

ESCAPE.

To the brook in the green meadow dancing,
   The tree-shaded, grass-bordered brook,
For a bath in its cool, limpid water,
   Old Dinah the baby boy took.

She drew off his cunning wee stockings,
   Unbuttoned each dainty pink shoe,
Untied the white slip and small apron,
   And loosened his petticoats, too.

And while Master Blue Eyes undressing,
    She told him in quaintest of words
Of the showers that came to the flowers,
    Of the rills that were baths for the birds.

And she said, "Dis yere sweetest of babies,
    W'en he's washed, jess as hansum'll be
As any red, yaller or blue bird
    Dat ebber singed up in a tree.

"An' sweeter den rosies an' lilies,
    Or wiolets eder, I guess—"
When away flew the mischievous darling,
    In the scantiest kind of a dress.

"Don't care if the birdies an' fowers,"
    He shouted, with clear, ringing laugh,
"Wash 'eir hands an' 'eir faces forebber
    An' ebber, *me* won't take a baff."

                        MARGARET EYTINGE.

ONE WAY TO BE BRAVE.

(*A True Story.*)

"**P**apa," exclaimed six-year-old Marland, leaning against his father's knee after listening to a true story, "I wish I could be as brave as that!"

"Perhaps you will be when you grow up."

"But maybe I sha'n't ever be on a railroad train when there is going to be an accident!"

"Ah! but there are sure to be plenty of other ways for a brave man to show himself."

Several days after this, when Marland had quite forgotten about trying to be brave, thinking, indeed, that he would have to wait anyway until he was a man, he and his little playmate, Ada, a year younger, were playing in the dog-kennel. It was a very large kennel, so that the two children often crept into it to "play house." After awhile, Marland, who, of course, was playing the papa of the house, was to go "down town" to his business; he put his little head out of the door of the kennel, and was just about to creep out, when right in front of him in the path he saw a snake. He knew in a moment just what sort of a snake it was, and how dangerous it was; he knew it was a rattlesnake, and that if it bit Ada or him, they would probably die. For Marland had spent two summers on his papa's big ranch in Kansas, and he had been told over and over again, if he ever saw a snake to run away from it as fast as he could, and this snake just in front of him was making the queer little noise with the rattles at the end of his tail which Marland had heard enough about to be able to recognize.

THE LITTLE RANCHMAN.
(From a photograph.)

Now you must know that a rattlesnake is not at all like a lion or a bear, although just as dangerous in its own way. It will not chase you; it can only spring a distance equal to its own length, and it has to wait and coil itself up in a ring, sounding its warning all the time, before it can strike at all. So if you are ever so little distance from it when you see it first, you can easily escape from it. The only danger is from stepping on it without seeing it. But Marland's snake was already coiled, and it was hardly more than a foot from the entrance to the kennel. You must know that the kennel was not out in an open field, either, but under a piazza, and a lattice work very near it left a very narrow passage for the children, even when there wasn't any snake. If they had been standing upright, they could have run, narrow as the way was; but they would have to crawl out of the kennel and find room for their entire little bodies on the ground before they could straighten themselves up and run. Fortunately, the snake's head was turned the other way.

"Ada," said Marland very quietly, so quietly that his grandpapa, raking the gravel on the walk near by, did not hear, him, "there's a snake out here, and it is a rattlesnake. Keep very still and crawl right after me."

"Yes, Ada," he whispered, as he succeeded in squirming himself out and wriggling past the snake till he could stand upright. "*There's room*, but you mustn't make any noise!"

Five minutes later the two children sauntered slowly down the avenue, hand in hand.

"Grandpapa," said Marland, "there's a rattlesnake in there where Ada and I were; perhaps you'd better kill him!"

And when the snake had been killed, and papa for the hundredth time had folded his little boy in his arms and murmured, "My brave boy! my dear, brave little boy!" Marland looked up in surprise.

"Why, it wasn't *I* that killed the snake, papa! it was grandpapa! I didn't do anything; I only kept very still and ran away!"

Listen, my children, and you shall hear
Of the midnight ride of Paul Revere,
On the eighteenth of April, in Seventy-Five:
Hardly a man is now alive
Who remembers that famous day and year.

He said to his friend—"If the British march
By land or sea from the town to-night,
Hang a lantern aloft in the belfry-arch
Of the North-Church tower, as a signal-light—
One if by land, and two if by sea;
And I on the opposite shore will be,
Ready to ride and spread the alarm
Through every Middlesex village and farm,
For the country-folk to be up and to arm."

Then he said good-night, and with muffled oar
Silently rowed to the Charlestown shore,
Just as the moon rose over the bay,
Where swinging wide at her moorings lay
The Somerset, British man-of-war:
A phantom ship, with each mast and spar
Across the moon, like a prison-bar,
And a huge, black hulk, that was magnified
By its own reflection in the tide.

Meanwhile, his friend, through alley and street
Wanders and watches with eager ears,

Till in the silence around him he hears
The muster of men at the barrack-door,
The sound of arms, and the tramp of feet,
And the measured tread of the grenadiers
Marching down to their boats on the shore.

Then he climbed to the tower of the church,
Up the wooden stairs, with stealthy tread,
To the belfry-chamber overhead,
And startled the pigeons from their perch
On the sombre rafters, that round him made
Masses and moving shapes of shade—
Up the light ladder, slender and tall,
To the highest window in the wall,
Where he paused to listen and look down
A moment on the roofs of the quiet town,
And the moonlight flowing over all.

Beneath, in the church-yard lay the dead
In their night-encampment on the hill,
Wrapped in silence so deep and still,
That he could hear, like a sentinel's tread
The watchful night-wind as it went
Creeping along from tent to tent,
And seeming to whisper, "All is well!"
A moment only he feels the spell
Of the place and the hour, the secret dread
Of the lonely belfry and the dead;
For suddenly all his thoughts are bent
On a shadowy something far away,
Where the river widens to meet the bay—
A line of black, that bends and floats
On the rising tide, like a bridge of boats.

Meanwhile, impatient to mount and ride,
Booted and spurred with a heavy stride,
On the opposite shore walked Paul Revere.
Now he patted his horse's side,
Now gazed on the landscape far and near,

Then impetuous stamped the earth,
And turned and tightened his saddle-girth;
But mostly he watched with eager search
The belfry-tower of the old North Church,
As it rose above the graves on the hill,
Lonely, and spectral, and sombre, and still.

And lo! as he looks, on the belfry's height,
A glimmer, and then a gleam of light!
He springs to the saddle, the bridle he turns,
But lingers and gazes, till full on his sight
A second lamp in the belfry burns.

A hurry of hoofs in a village-street,
A shape in the moonlight, a bulk in the dark,
And beneath from the pebbles, in passing, a spark
Struck out by a steed that flies fearless and fleet:
That was all! And yet, through the gloom and the light,
The fate of a nation was riding that night;
And the spark struck out by that steed, in his flight,
Kindled the land into flame with its heat.

It was twelve by the village-clock,
When he crossed the bridge into Medford town,
He heard the crowing of the cock,
And the barking of the farmer's dog,
And felt the damp of the river-fog,
That rises when the sun goes down.

It was one by the village-clock,
When he rode into Lexington.
He saw the gilded weathercock
Swim in the moonlight as he passed,
And the meeting-house windows, blank and bare,
Gaze at him with a spectral glare,
As if they already stood aghast
At the bloody work they would look upon.

It was two by the village-clock,

When he came to the bridge in Concord town.
He heard the bleating of the flock,
And the twitter of birds among the trees,
And felt the breath of the morning-breeze
Blowing over the meadows brown.
And one was safe and asleep in his bed,
Who at the bridge would be first to fall,
Who that day would be lying dead,
Pierced by a British musket-ball.

You know the rest. In the books you have read
How the British regulars fired and fled—
How the farmers gave them ball for ball,
From behind each fence and farmyard-wall,
Chasing the red-coats down the lane,
Then crossing the fields to emerge again
Under the trees at the turn of the road,
And only pausing to fire and load.

So through the night rode Paul Revere;
And so through the night went his cry of alarm
To every Middlesex village and farm—
A cry of defiance, and not of fear—
A voice in the darkness, a knock at the door,
And a word that shall echo for evermore!
For, borne on the night-wind of the Past,
Through all our history, to the last,
In the hour of darkness, and peril, and need,
The people will waken and listen to hear
The hurrying hoof-beat of that steed,
And the midnight-message of Paul Revere.

HENRY WADSWORTH LONGFELLOW.

TWO PERSIAN SCHOOLBOYS.

"Wake, Otanes, wake, the Magi are singing the morning hymn to Mithras. Quick, or we shall be late at the exercises, and father promised, if we did well, we should go to the chase with him to-day."

"And perhaps shoot a lion. What a feather in our caps that would be! Is it pleasant?"

Smerdis pulled open the shutters that closed the windows, and the first rays of the sun sparkled on the trees and fountains of a beautiful garden beyond whose lofty walls appeared the dwellings and towers of a mighty city. Already the low roar of its traffic reached them while hurrying on their clothes to join their companions in the spacious grounds where they were trained in wrestling, throwing blocks of wood at each other to acquire agility in dodging the missiles, the skilful use of the bow, and various other exercises for the development of bodily strength and grace.

A few minutes later the two brothers, Smerdis and Otanes, with scores of other lads, ranging in age from seven to fourteen years, were assembled in a vast playground, surrounded on all sides by a lofty wall.

The playground of a large boarding-school?

It almost might be called so, but the pupils of this boarding-school were educated free of expense to their parents, and it received only the sons of the highest nobles in the land. This playground was attached to the palace of Darius, King of Persia, who reigned twenty-four hundred years ago, and these chosen boys had been taken from their homes, as they reached the age of six years, to be reared "at his gate," as the language of the country expressed it.

Otanes and Smerdis were sons of one of the highest officers of the court, the "ear of the king," or, as he would now be called, the Minister of Police. Handsome little fellows of eleven and twelve, with blue eyes, fair complexions, and curling yellow locks, their long training in all sorts of physical exercises had made them stronger and hardier than most lads of their age in our time. Though reared in a palace, at one of the most splendid courts the world has ever seen, the boys were expected to endure the hardships of the poorest laborer's children. Instead of the gold and silver bedsteads used by the nobles, they were obliged to sleep on the floor; if the court was at Babylon, they were forced to make long marches under the burning sun of Asia, and if, to escape the intense heat, the king removed to his summer palaces at Ecbatana and Pasargadæ, situated in the mountainous regions of Persia, where it was often bitterly cold, the boys were ordered to bathe in the icy water of the rivers flowing from the heights. In place of the dainty dishes and sweetmeats for which Persian cooks were famous, they were allowed nothing but bread, water, and a little meat; sometimes to accustom them to hardships they were deprived entirely of food for a day or even longer.

THE BOYS HURRIED OFF TOWARD HOME.

On this morning the exercises seemed specially long to the two brothers, full of anticipations of pleasure; but finally the last block of wood was hurled, the last arrow shot, the last wrestling match ended, and the boys, bearing a sealed roll of papyrus, containing a leave of absence for one day, hurried off towards home.

Their father's palace stood at no great distance from the royal residence, on the long, wide street extending straight to the city gates, and like the houses of all the Persian nobles, was surrounded by a beautiful walled garden called a paradise, laid out with flower-beds of roses, poppies, oleanders, ornamental plants, adorned with fountains, and shaded by lofty trees.

The hunting party was nearly ready to start, and the courtyard was thronged. Servants rushed to and fro bearing shields, swords, lances, bows and lassos, for a hunter was always equipped with bow and arrows, two lances, a sword and a shield. Others held in leash the dogs to be used in starting the game.

The enormous preserves in the neighborhood of Babylon were well stocked with animals, including stags, wild boars, and a few lions. Several noblemen clad in the plain hunting costume always worn in the chase, were already mounted, among them the father of the two lads, who greeted them affectionately as they respectfully approached and kissed his hand.

"Make haste, boys, your horses are ready. Take only bows and shields—the swords and lances will be in your way; you must not try to deal with larger game than you can manage with your arrows."

"May we not carry daggers in our belts, too, father?" cried Otanes eagerly. "They can't be in our way, and if we should meet a lion—"

A laugh from the group of nobles interrupted him. "Your son seeks large game, Intaphernes!" exclaimed a handsome officer. "He must have better weapons than a bow and dagger, if—"

The rest of the sentence was drowned by the noise in the courtyard, but as the party rode towards the gate Intaphernes looked back: "Yes, take the daggers, it can do no harm. Keep with Candaules."

The old slave, a gray-haired, but muscular man, with several other attendants, joined the lads, and the long train passed out into the street and toward the city gates. Otanes hastily whispered to his brother: "Keep close by me, Smerdis; if only we catch sight of a lion, we'll show what we can do with bows and arrows."

The sun was now several hours high, and the streets, lined with tall brick houses, were crowded with people—artisans, slaves, soldiers, nobles and citizens, the latter clad in white linen shirts, gay woollen tunics and short cloaks. Two-wheeled wooden vehicles, drawn by horses decked with bells and tassels, litters containing veiled women borne by slaves, and now and then, the superb gilded carriage, hung with silk curtains, of some royal princess passed along. Here and there a heavily laden camel moved slowly by, and the next instant a soldier of the king's bodyguard dashed past in his superb uniform—a gold cuirass, purple surcoat, and high Persian cap, the gold scabbard of his sword and the gold apple on his lance-tip flashing in the sun.

THE HUNTING PARTY WERE NEARLY READY TO START.

High above the topmost roofs of even the lofty towers on the walls rose the great sanctuary of the Magi,[1] the immense Temple of Bel, visible in all quarters of the city, and seen for miles from every part of the flat plain on which Babylon stood. The huge staircase wound like a serpent round and round the outside of the building to the highest story, which contained the sanctuary itself and also the observatory whence the priests studied the stars.

Otanes and Smerdis, chatting eagerly together, rode on as fast as the crowd would permit, and soon reached one of the gates in the huge walls that defended the city. These walls, seventy-five feet high, and wide enough to allow two chariots to drive abreast, were strengthened by two hundred and fifty towers, except on one side, where deep marshes extended to their base. Beyond these marshes lay the hunting-grounds, and the party, turning to the left, rode for a time over a smooth highway, between broad tracts of land sown with wheat, barley and sesame. Slender palm-trees covered with clusters of golden dates were seen in every direction, and the sunbeams shimmered on the canals and ditches which conducted water from the Euphrates to all parts of the fields.

Otanes' horse suddenly shied violently as a rider, mounted on a fleet steed, and carrying a large pouch, dashed by like the wind.

"One of the Augari bearing letters to the next station!" exclaimed Smerdis. "See how he skims along. Hi! If I were not to be one of the king's bodyguard, I'd try for an Augar's place. How he goes! He's almost out of sight already."

"How far apart are the stations?" asked Otanes.

"Eighteen miles. And when he gets there, he'll just toss the letter bag to the next man, who is sitting on a fresh horse waiting for it, and away *he'll* go like lightning. That's the way the news is carried to the very end of the empire of our lord the King."

"Must be fine fun," replied Otanes. "But see, there's the gate of the hunting-park. Now for the lion," he added gayly.

"May Ormuzd[2] save you from meeting one, my young master," said the old servant, Candaules. "Luckily it's broad daylight, and they are more apt to come from their lairs after dark. Better begin with smaller game and leave the lion and wild boars to your father."

"Not if we catch sight of them," cried Otanes, settling his shield more firmly on his arm, and urging his horse to a quicker pace, for the head of the long train of attendants had already disappeared amid the dark cypress-trees of the hunting park. The immense enclosure stretching from the edge of the morasses that bordered the walls of Babylon far into the country, soon echoed with the shouts of the attendants beating the coverts for game, the baying of the dogs, the hiss of lances and whir of arrows. Bright-hued birds, roused by the tumult, flew wildly hither and thither, now and then the superb plumage of a bird of paradise flashing like a jewel among the dense foliage of cypress and nut-trees.

Hour after hour sped swiftly away; the party had dispersed in different directions, following the course of the game; the sun was sinking low, and the slaves were bringing the slaughtered birds and beasts to the wagons used to convey them home. A magnificent stag was among the spoil, and a fierce wild boar, after a long struggle, had fallen under a thrust from Intaphernes's lance.

The shrill blast of the Median trumpet sounded thrice, to give the first of the three signals for the scattered hunters to meet at the appointed place, near the entrance of the park, and the two young brothers who, attended by Candaules and half a dozen slaves, had ridden far into the shady recesses of the woods, reluctantly turned their horses' heads. No thought of disobeying the summons entered their minds—Persian boys were taught that next to truth and courage, obedience was the highest virtue, and rarely was a command transgressed.

They had had a good day's sport; few arrows remained in their quivers, and the attendants carried bunches of gay plumaged birds and several small animals, among them a pretty little fawn. "Let's go nearer the marshes; there are not so many trees, and we can ride faster," said Otanes as the trumpet-call was repeated, and the little party turned in that direction, moving more swiftly as they passed out upon the strip of open ground between the thicket and the marshes. The sun was just setting. The last crimson rays, shimmering on the pools of water standing here and there in the morasses, cast reflections on the tall reeds and rushes bordering their margins.

Suddenly a pretty spotted fawn darted in front of the group, and crossing the open ground, vanished amid a thick clump of reeds. "What a nice pet the little creature would make for our sister Hadassah!" cried Otanes eagerly. "See! it has hidden among the reeds; we might take it alive. Go with Candaules and the slaves, Smerdis, and form a half-circle beyond the clump. When you're ready, whistle, and I'll ride straight down and drive it towards you; you can easily catch it then. We are so near the entrance of the park now that we shall have plenty of time; the third signal hasn't sounded yet."

Smerdis instantly agreed to the plan. The horses were fastened to some trees, and the men cautiously made a wide circuit, passed the bed of reeds, and concealed themselves, behind the tall rushes beyond. A low whistle gave Otanes the signal to drive out the fawn.

Smerdis and the slaves saw the lad straighten himself in the saddle, and with a shout, dash at full speed towards the spot where the fawn had vanished. He had almost reached it when the stiff stalks shook violently, and a loud roar made them all spring to their feet. They saw the brave boy check his horse and fit an arrow to the string, but as he drew the bow, there was a stronger rustle among the reeds; a tawny object flashed through the air, striking Otanes from his saddle, while the horse free from its rider, dashed, snorting with terror, towards the park entrance.

"A lion! A lion!" shrieked the trembling slaves, but Smerdis, drawing his dagger, ran towards the place where his brother had fallen, passing close by the body of the fawn which lay among the reeds with its head crushed by a blow from the lion's paw. Candaules followed close at the lad's heels.

Parting the thick growth of stalks, they saw, only a few paces off, Otanes, covered with blood, lying motionless on the ground, and beside him the dead body of a half-grown lion, the boy's arrow buried in one eye, while the blood still streamed from the lance-wound in the animal's side.

Smerdis, weeping, threw himself beside his brother, and at the same moment Intaphernes, with several nobles and attendants, attracted by the cries, dashed up to the spot. The father, springing from the saddle, bent, and laid his hand on the boy's heart.

"It is beating still, and strongly too," he exclaimed. "Throw water in his face! perhaps—"

Without finishing the sentence, he carefully examined the motionless form. "Ormuzd be praised! He has no wound; the blood has flowed from the lion. See, Prexaspes, there is a lance-head sticking in its side. I believe it's the very beast you wounded early in the day."

The officer whose laugh had so vexed Otanes, stooped over the dead lion and looked at the broken shaft.

"Ay, it's my weapon; the beast probably made its way to the morass for water; but, by Mithras![3] the lad's arrow killed the brute; the barb passed through the eyeball into the brain."

"Yes, my lord," cried old Candaules eagerly, "and doubtless it was only the weight of the animal, which, striking my young master as it made its spring, hurled him from the saddle and stunned him. See! he is opening his eyes. Otanes, Otanes, you've killed the lion!"

The boy's eyelids fluttered, then slowly rose, his eyes wandered over the group, and at last rested on the dead lion. The old slave's words had evidently reached his ear, for with a faint smile he glanced archly at Prexaspes, and raising himself on one elbow, said:

"You see, my lord—even with a bow and dagger!"

MARY J. SAFFORD.

Footnote 1: (return)

The Magi were the Persian priests.

Footnote 2: (return)

The principal god of the Persians.

Footnote 3: (return)

The Persian god of the sun.

DO YOU KNOW HIM?

COULDN'T BEAR TO BE LAUGHED AT.

There was once a small boy—he might measure four feet;

His conduct was perfectly splendid,
His manners were good, and his temper was sweet,
His teeth and his hair were uncommonly neat,
    In fact he could not be amended.

His smile was so bright, and his word was so kind,
    His hand was so quick to assist it,
His wits were so clever, his air so refined,
There was something so nice in him, body and mind,
    That you never could try to resist it.

THE WEAVER OF BRUGES.

The strange old streets of Bruges town
    Lay white with dust and summer sun,
The tinkling goat bells slowly passed
    At milking-time, ere day was done.

An ancient weaver, at his loom,
    With trembling hands his shuttle plied,
While roses grew beneath his touch,
    And lovely hues were multiplied.

The slant sun, through the open door,
    Fell bright, and reddened warp and woof,
When with a cry of pain a little bird,
    A nestling stork, from off the roof,

Sore wounded, fluttered in and sat
    Upon the old man's outstretched hand;
"Dear Lord," he murmured, under breath,
    "Hast thou sent me this little friend?"

And to his lonely heart he pressed
    The little one, and vowed no harm
Should reach it there; so, day by day,
    Caressed and sheltered by his arm,

The young stork grew apace, and from
    The loom's high beams looked down with eyes
Of silent love upon his ancient friend,
    As two lone ones might sympathize.

At last the loom was hushed: no more
    The deftly handled shuttle flew;
No more the westering sunlight fell
    Where blushing silken roses grew.

And through the streets of Bruges town
    By strange hands cared for, to his last
And lonely rest, 'neath darkening skies,

The ancient weaver slowly passed;

Then strange sight met the gaze of all:
   A great white stork, with wing-beats slow,
Too sad to leave the friend he loved,
   With drooping head, flew circling low,

And ere the trampling feet had left
   The new-made mound, dropt slowly down,
And clasped the grave in his white wings
   His pure breast on the earth so brown.

Nor food, nor drink, could lure him thence,
   Sunrise nor fading sunsets red;
When little children came to see,
   The great white stork—was dead.

M.M.P. DINSMOOR.

THE MAN IN THE TUB.

Come here, little folks, while I rub and I rub!
O, there once was a man who lived in a tub,
In a classical town far over the seas;
The name of this fellow was Diogenes.

And this is the story: it happened one day
That a wonderful king came riding that way;
Said he, to the man in the tub, "How d'ye do?
I'm Great Alexander; now, pray, who are you?"

O, yes, to be clean you must rub, you must rub!
Though he lived and he slept and ate in a tub,
This singular man, in towns where he halted,
History tells us was greatly exalted.

He rose in his tub: "I am Diogenes."
"Dear me," quoth the king, who'd been over the seas,
"I've heard of you often; now, what can I do
To aid such a wise individual as you?"

Could one expect manners, I ask, as I rub,
From a man quite content to live in a tub?
"Get out of my sunlight," growled Diogenes
To this affable king who'd been o'er the seas.

MAY E. STONE.

THE LITTLE GOLD MINERS OF THE SIERRAS.

Their mother had died crossing the plains, and their father had had a leg broken by a wagon wheel passing over it as they descended the Sierras, and he was for a long time after reaching the mines miserable, lame and poor.

The eldest boy, Jim Keene, as I remember him, was a bright little fellow, but wild as an Indian and full of mischief. The next eldest child, Madge, was a girl of ten, her father's favorite, and she was wild enough too. The youngest was Stumps. Poor, timid, starved Little Stumps! I never knew his real name. But he was the baby, and hardly yet out of petticoats. And he was very short in the legs, very short in the body, very short in the arms and neck; and so he was called Stumps because he looked it. In fact he seemed to have stopped growing entirely. Oh, you don't know how hard the old Plains were on everybody, when we crossed them in ox-wagons, and it took more than half a year to make the journey. The little children, those that did not die, turned brown like the Indians, in that long, dreadful journey of seven months, and stopped growing for a time.

For the first month or two after reaching the Sierras, old Mr. Keene limped about among the mines trying to learn the mystery of finding gold, and the art of digging. But at last, having grown strong enough, he went to work for wages, to get bread for his half-wild little ones, for they were destitute indeed.

Things seemed to move on well, then. Madge cooked the simple meals, and Little Stumps clung to her dress with his little pinched brown hand wherever she went, while Jim whooped it over the hills and chased jack-rabbits as if he were a greyhound. He would climb trees, too, like a squirrel. And, oh!—it was deplorable—but how he could swear!

At length some of the miners, seeing the boy must come to some bad end if not taken care of, put their heads and their pockets together and sent the children to school. This school was a mile away over the beautiful brown hills, a long, pleasant walk under the green California oaks.

Well, Jim would take the little tin dinner bucket, and his slate, and all their books under his arm and go booming ahead about half a mile in advance, while Madge with brown Little Stumps clinging to her side like a burr, would come stepping along the trail under the oak-trees as fast as she could after him.

But if a jack-rabbit, or a deer, or a fox crossed Jim's path, no matter how late it was, or how the teacher had threatened him, he would drop books, lunch, slate and all, and spitting on his hands and rolling up his sleeves, would bound away after it, yelling like a wild Indian. And some days, so fascinating was the chase, Jim did not appear at the schoolhouse at all; and of course Madge and Stumps played truant too. Sometimes a week together would pass and the Keene children would not be seen at the schoolhouse. Visits from the schoolmaster produced no lasting effect. The children would come for a day or two, then be seen no more. The schoolmaster and their father at last had a serious talk about the matter.

"What *can* I do with him?" said Mr. Keene.

"You'll have to put him to work," said the schoolmaster. "Set him to hunting nuggets instead of bird's-nests. I guess what the boy wants is some honest means of using his strength. He's a good boy, Mr. Keene; don't despair of him. Jim would be proud to be an 'honest miner.' Jim's a good boy, Mr. Keene."

"Well, then, thank you, Schoolmaster," said Mr. Keene. "Jim's a good boy; and Madge is good, Mr. Schoolmaster; and poor starved and stunted motherless Little Stumps, he is good as gold, Mr. Schoolmaster. And I want to be a mother to 'em—I want to be father and mother to 'em all, Mr. Schoolmaster. And I'll follow your advice. I'll put 'em all to work a-huntin' for gold."

The next day away up on the hillside under a pleasant oak, where the air was sweet and cool, and the ground soft and dotted over with flowers, the tender-hearted old man that wanted to be "father and mother both," "located" a claim. The flowers were kept fresh by a little stream of waste water from the ditch that girded the brow of the hill above. Here he set a sluice-box and put his three little miners at work with pick, pan and shovel. There he left them and limped back to his own place in the mine below.

And how they did work! And how pleasant it was here under the broad boughs of the oak, with the water rippling through the sluice on the soft, loose soil which they shoveled into the long sluice-box. They could see the mule-trains going and coming, and the clouds of dust far below which told them the stage was whirling up the valley. But Jim kept steadily on at his work day after day. Even though jack-rabbits and squirrels appeared on the very scene, he would not leave till, like the rest of the honest miners, he could shoulder his pick and pan and go down home with the setting sun.

Sometimes the men who had tried to keep the children at school, would come that way, and with a sly smile, talk very wisely about whether or not the new miners would "strike it" under the cool oak among the flowers on the hill. But Jim never stopped to talk much. He dug and wrestled away, day after day, now up to his waist in the pit.

One Saturday evening the old man limped up the hillside to help the young miners "clean up."

"COLOR! TWO COLORS! THREE, FOUR, FIVE—A DOZEN!"

He sat down at the head of the sluice-box and gave directions how they should turn off the most of the water, wash down the "toilings" very low, lift up the "riffle," brush down the "apron," and finally set the pan in the lower end of the "sluice-toil" and pour in the quicksilver to gather up and hold the gold.

"What for you put your hand in de water for, papa?" queried Little Stumps, who had left off his work, which consisted mainly of pulling flowers and putting them in the sluice-box to see them float away. He was sitting by his father's side, and he looked up in his face as he spoke.

"Hush, child," said the old man softly, as he again dipped his thumb and finger in his vest pocket as if about to take snuff. But he did not take snuff. Again his hand was reached down to the rippling water at the head of the sluice-box. And this time curious but obedient Little Stumps was silent.

Suddenly there was a shout, such a shout from Jim as the hills had not heard since he was a schoolboy.

He had found the "color." "Two colors! three, four, five—a dozen!" The boy shouted like a Modoc, threw down the brush and scraper, and kissed his little sister over and over, and cried as he did so; then he whispered softly to her as he again took up his brush and scraper, that it was "for papa; all for poor papa; that he did not care for himself, but he did want to help poor, tired, and crippled papa." But papa did not seem to be excited so very much.

The little miners were now continually wild with excitement. They were up and at work Monday morning at dawn. The men who were in the father's tender secret, congratulated the children heartily and made them presents of several small nuggets to add to their little hoard.

In this way they kept steadily at work for half the summer. All the gold was given to papa to keep. Papa weighed it each week, and I suppose secretly congratulated himself that he was getting back about as much as he put in.

Before quite the end of the third month, Jim struck a thin bed of blue gravel. The miners who had been happily chuckling and laughing among themselves to think how they had managed to keep Jim out of mischief, began to look at each other and wonder how in the world blue gravel ever got up there on the hill. And in a few days more there was a well-defined bed of blue gravel, too; and not one of the miners could make it out.

One Saturday evening shortly after, as the old man weighed their gold he caught his breath, started, and stood up straight; straighter than he had stood since he crossed the Plains. Then he hastily left the cabin. He went up the hill to the children's claim almost without limping. Then he took a pencil and an old piece of a letter, and wrote out a notice and tacked it up on the big oak-tree, claiming those mining claims according to miners' law, for the three children. A couple of miners laughed as they went by in the twilight, to see what he was doing; and he laughed with them. But as he limped on down the hill he smiled.

That night as they sat at supper, he told the children that as they had been such faithful and industrious miners, he was going to give them each a present, besides a little gold to spend as they pleased.

So he went up to the store and bought Jim a red shirt, long black and bright gum boots, a broad-brimmed hat, and a belt. He also bought each of the other children some pretty trappings, and gave each a dollar's worth of gold dust. Madge and Stumps handed their gold back to "poor papa." But Jim was crazy with excitement. He put on his new clothes and went forth to spend his dollar. And what do you suppose he bought? I hesitate to tell you. But what he bought was a pipe and a paper of tobacco!

That red shirt, that belt and broad-brimmed hat, together with the shiny top boots, had been too much for Jim's balance. How could a man—he spoke of himself as a man now—how could a man be an "honest miner" and not smoke a pipe?

And now with his manly clothes and his manly pipe he was to be so happy! He had all that went to make up "the honest miner." True, he did not let his father know about the pipe. He hid it under his pillow at night. He meant to have his first smoke at the sluice-box, as a miner should.

Monday morning he was up with the sun and ready for his work. His father, who worked down the Gulch, had already gone before the children had finished their breakfast. So now Jim filled his bran-new pipe very leisurely;

and with as much calm unconcern as if he had been smoking for forty years, he stopped to scratch a match on the door as he went out.

From under his broad hat he saw his little sister watching him, and he fairly swelled with importance as Stumps looked up at him with childish wonder. Leaving Madge to wash the few tin dishes and follow as she could with Little Stumps, he started on up the hill, pipe in mouth.

He met several miners, but he puffed away like a tug-boat against the tide, and went on. His bright new boots whetted and creaked together, the warm wind lifted the broad brim of his *sombrero*, and his bright new red shirt was really beautiful, with the green grass and oaks for a background—and so this brave young man climbed the hill to his mine. Ah, he was so happy!

Suddenly, as he approached the claim, his knees began to smite together, and he felt so weak he could hardly drag one foot after the other. He threw down his pick; he began to tremble and spin around. The world seemed to be turning over and over, and he trying in vain to hold on to it. He jerked the pipe from his teeth, and throwing it down on the bank, he tumbled down too, and clutching at the grass with both hands tried hard, oh! so hard, to hold the world from slipping from under him.

"Oh, Jim! you are white as snow," cried Madge as she came up.

"White as 'er sunshine, an' blue, an' green too, sisser. Look at brurrer 'all colors,'" piped Little Stumps pitifully.

"O, Jim, Jim—brother Jim, what is the matter?" sobbed Madge.

"Sunstroke," murmured the young man, smiling grimly, like a true Californian. "No; it is not sunstroke, it's—it's cholera," he added in dismay over his falsehood.

Poor boy! he was sorry for this second lie too. He fairly groaned in agony of body and soul.

Oh, how he did hate that pipe! How he did want to get up and jump on it and smash it into a thousand pieces! But he could not get up or turn around or move at all without betraying his unmanly secret.

A couple of miners came up, but Jim feebly begged them to go.

"Sunstroke," whispered the sister.

"No; tolera," piped poor Little Stumps.

"Get out! Leave me!" groaned the young red-shirted miner of the Sierras.

The biggest of the two miners bent over him a moment.

"Yes; it's both," he muttered. "Cholera-nicotine-fantum!" Then he looked at his partner and winked wickedly. Without a word, he took the limp young miner up in his arms and bore him down the hill to his father's cabin, while Stumps and Madge ran along at either side, and tenderly and all the time kept asking what was good for "cholera."

The other old "honest miner" lingered behind to pick up the baleful pipe which he knew was somewhere there; and when the little party was far enough down the hill, he took it up and buried it in his own capacious pocket with a half-sorrowful laugh. "Poor little miner," he sighed.

"Don't ever swear any more, Windy," pleaded the boy to the miner who had carried him down the hill, as he leaned over him, "and don't never lie. I am going to die, Windy, and I should like to be good. Windy, it *ain't* sunstroke, it's" ...

HE TOOK THE LIMP YOUNG MINER IN HIS ARMS.

"Hush yer mouth," growled Windy. "I know what 'tis! We've left it on the hill."

The boy turned his face to the wall. The conviction was strong upon him that he was going to die, The world spun round now very, very fast indeed. Finally, half-rising in bed, he called Little Stumps to his side:

"Stumps, dear, good Little Stumps, if I die don't you never try for to smoke; for that's what's the matter with me. No, Stumps—dear little brother Stumps—don't you never try for to go the whole of the 'honest miner,' for it can't be did by a boy! We're nothing but boys, you and I, Stumps—Little Stumps."

He sank back in bed and Little Stumps and his sister cried and cried, and kissed him and kissed him.

The miners who had gathered around loved him now, every one, for daring to tell the truth and take the shame of his folly so bravely.

"I'm going to die, Windy," groaned the boy.

Windy could stand no more of it. He took Jim's hand with a cheery laugh. "Git well in half an hour," said he, "now that you've out with the truth."

And so he did. By the time his father came home he was sitting up; and he ate breakfast the next morning as if nothing had happened. But he never tried to smoke any more as long as he lived. And he never lied, and he never swore any more.

Oh, no! this Jim that I have been telling you of is "Moral Jim," of the Sierras. The mine? Oh, I almost forgot. Well, that blue dirt was the old bed of the stream, and it was ten times richer than where the miners were all at work below. Struck it! I should say so! Ask any of the old Sierras miners about "The Children's Claim," if you want to hear just how rich they struck it.

JOAQUIN MILLER.

OLD GODFREY'S RELIC.

A simple, upright man was he,
 Of spirit undefiled,
Cheerful and hale at seventy-three,
 As any blithesome child.

Old Godfrey's friends and neighbors felt
 His due was honest praise;
Ofttimes how fervently they dwelt
 On his brave words and ways!

He had no foeman in the land
 Whose deeds or tongue would gall;
Of guileless heart, of liberal hand,
 He smiled on one and all.

But most, I think, he smiled on me;
 "Your eyes, dear boy," he said,
"Remind me, though not mournfully,
 Of eyes whose light is dead."

How oft beneath his roof I've been
 On eves of wintry blight,
And heard his magic violin
 Make musical the night.

No consort by his board was set,
 No child his hearth had known,
Yet of all souls I've ever met,
 His seemed the least alone.

What stories in my eager ears
    He poured of peace or strife;
Keen memories of the thrilling years
    That thronged his ocean life.

And oh, he showed such marvellous things
    From unknown sea and shore,
That, brimmed with strange imaginings,
    My boy's brain bubbled o'er!

It wandered back o'er many a track
    Of his old life-toil free;
The enchanted calm, the fiery wrack,
    Far off, far off at sea!

For once he dared the watery world,
    O'er wild or halcyon waves,
And saw his snow-white sails unfurled
    Above a million graves.

Northward he went, thro' ice and sleet,
    Where soon the sunbeams fail,
And followed with an armed fleet
    The wide wake of the whale.

Southward he went through airs serene
    Of soft Sicilian noon,
And sang, on level decks, between
    The twilight and the moon.

But once—it was a tranquil time,
    An evening half divine,
When the low breeze like murmurous rhyme
    Sighed through the sunset fine.

Once, Godfrey from the secret place
    Wherein his treasures lay,
Brought forth, with calmly museful face,

This relic to the day—

A soft tress with a silken tie,
    A brightly shimmering curl;
Such as might shadow goldenly
    The fair brow of a girl.

"Oh, lovelier," cried I, "than the dawn
    Auroral mists enfold,
The long and luminous threadlets drawn
    Through this rich curl of gold!

"Tell, tell me, o'er whose graceful head
    You saw the ringlet shine?"
Thereon the old man coolly said,
    "Why, lad, the tress is mine!

"Look not amazed, but come with me,
    And let me tell you where
And how, one morning fearfully,
    I lost that lock of hair."

He led me past his cottage screen
    Of flowers, far down the wood
Where, towering o'er the landscape green,
    A centuried oak-tree stood.

"Here is the place," he said, "whereon
    Heaven helped me in sore strait,
And in a March morn's radiance wan
    Turned back the edge of fate!

"My father a stout yeoman was,
    And I, in childish pride,
That morning through the dew-drenched grass,
    Walked gladly by his side,

"Till *here* he paused, with glittering steel,
    A prostrate trunk to smite;

How the near woodland seemed to reel
    Beneath his blows of might!

"And round about me viciously
    The splinters flashed and flew;
Some sharply grazed the shuddering eye,
    Some pattered down the dew.

"Childlike, I strove to pick them up,
    But stumbling forward, sunk,
O'er the wild pea and buttercup,
    Across the smitten trunk.

"Just then, with all its ponderous force
    The axe was hurtling down;
What spell could stay its savage course?
    What charm could save my crown?

"Too late, too late to stop the blow;
    I shrieked to see it come;
My father's blood grew cold as snow;
    My father's voice was dumb.

"He staggered back a moment's space,
    Glaring on earth and skies;
Blank horror in his haggard face,
    Dazed anguish in his eyes.

"He searched me close to find my wound;
    He searched with sobbing breath;
But not the smallest gateway found
    Opened to welcome death.

"He thanked his God in ardent wise,
    Kneeling 'twixt shine and shade;
Then lowered his still half-moistened eyes
    O'er the keen axe's blade.

"*Two hairs clung to it!*... thence, he turned

Where the huge log had rolled,
And there in tempered sunlight burned
   A quivering curl of gold.

"The small thing looked alive!... it stirred
   By breeze and sunbeam kissed,
And fluttered like an Orient bird,
   Half-glimpsed through sunrise mist.

"Oh! keen and sheer the axe-edge smote
   The perfect curl apart!
Even *now*, through tingling head and throat,
   I feel the old terror dart.

"My father kept his treasure long,
   'Mid seasons grave or gay,
Till to death's plaintive curfew-song,
   Calmly he passed away.

"I, too, the token still so fair,
   Have held with tendance true;
And dying, this memorial hair
   I'll leave, dear lad, to you!"

PAUL H. HAYNE.

EVAN COGWELL'S ICE FORT.

In the early days of Northern Ohio, when settlers were few and far between, Evan Cogswell, a Welsh lad of sixteen years, found his way thither and began his career as a laborer, receiving at first but two dollars a month in addition to his board and "home-made" clothing. He possessed an intelligent, energetic mind in a sound and vigorous body, and had acquired in his native parish the elements of an education in both Welsh and English.

The story of his life, outlined in a curious old diary containing the records of sixty-two years, and an entry for more than twenty-two thousand days, would constitute a history of the region, and some of its passages would read like high-wrought romance.

His first term of service was with a border farmer on the banks of a stream called Grand River, in Ashtabula County. It was rather crude farming, however, consisting mostly of felling trees, cutting wood and saw-logs, burning brush, and digging out stumps, the axe and pick-axe finding more use than ordinary farm implements.

Seven miles down the river, and on the opposite bank, lived the nearest neighbors, among them a blacksmith who in his trade served the whole country for twenty miles around. One especial part of his business was the repairing of axes, called in that day "jumping," or "upsetting."

In midwinter Evan's employer left a couple of axes with the blacksmith for repairs, the job to be done within a week. At this time the weather was what is termed "settled," with deep snow, and good "slipping" along the few wildwood roads.

But three or four days later, there came a "January thaw." Rain and a warmer temperature melted away much of the snow, the little river was swelled to a great torrent, breaking up the ice and carrying it down stream, and the roads became almost impassable. When the week was up and the farmer wanted the axes, it was not possible for the horse to travel, and after waiting vainly for a day or two for a turn in the weather, Evan was posted off on foot to obtain the needed implements. Delighting in the change and excitement of such a trip, the boy started before noon, expecting to reach home again ere dark, as it was not considered quite safe to journey far by night on account of the wolves.

Three miles below, at a narrow place in the river, was the bridge, consisting of three very long tree-trunks reaching parallel from bank to bank, and covered with hewn plank. When Evan arrived here he found that this bridge had been swept away. But pushing on down stream among the thickets, about half a mile below, he came upon an immense ice-jam, stretching across the stream and piled many feet high. Upon this he at once resolved to make his way over to the road on the other side, for he was already wearied threading the underbrush. Grand River, which is a narrow but deep and violent stream, ran roaring and plunging beneath the masses of ice as if enraged at being so obstructed; but the lad picked his path in safety and soon stood on the opposite bank.

Away he hurried now to the blacksmith's, so as to complete his errand and return by this precarious crossing before dark.

But the smith had neglected his duty and Evan had to wait an hour or more for the axes. At length they were done, and with one tied at each end of a strong cord and this hung about his neck, he was off on the homeward trip. To aid his walking, he procured from the thicket a stout cane. He had hardly gone two miles when the duskiness gathering in the woods denoted the nearness of night; yet as the moon was riding high, he pushed on without fear.

HOMEWARD.   SAFELY INTRENCHED.

But as he was skirting a wind-fall of trees, he came suddenly upon two or three
wolves apparently emerging from their daytime hiding place for a hunting

expedition. Evan was considerably startled; but as they ran off into the woods as if afraid of him, he took courage in the hope that they would not molest him. In a few minutes, however, they set up that dismal howling by which they summon their mates and enlarge their numbers; and Evan discovered by the sounds that they were following him cautiously at no great distance.

Frequent responses were also heard from more distant points in the woods and from across the river. By this time it was becoming quite dark, the moonlight penetrating the forest only along the roadway and in occasional patches among the trees on either side. The rushing river was not far away, but above its roar arose every instant the threatening howl of a wolf. Finally, just as he reached the ice-bridge, the howling became still, a sign that their numbers emboldened them to enter in earnest on the pursuit. The species of wolf once so common in the central States, and making the early farmers so much trouble, were peculiar in this respect; they were great cowards singly, and would trail the heels of a traveler howling for recruits, and not daring to begin the attack until they had collected a force that insured success; then they became fierce and bold, and more to be dreaded than any other animal of the wilderness. And at this point, when they considered their numbers equal to the occasion, the howling ceased.

Evan had been told of this, and when the silence began, he knew its meaning, and his heart shuddered at the prospect. His only hope lay in the possibility that they might not dare to follow him across the ice-bridge. But this hope vanished as he approached the other shore, and saw by the moonlight several of the gaunt creatures awaiting him on that side. What should he do? No doubt they would soon muster boldness to follow him upon the ice, and then his fate would be sealed in a moment.

In the emergency he thought of the axes, and taking them from his neck, cut the cord, and thrust his walking-stick into one as a helve, resolved to defend himself to the last.

At this instant he espied among the thick, upheaved ice-cakes two great fragments leaning against each other in such a way as to form a roof with something like a small room underneath. Here he saw his only chance. Springing within, he used the axe to chip off other fragments with which to close up the entrance, and almost quicker than it can be told, had thus constructed a sort of fort, which he believed would withstand the attack of the wolves. At nightfall the weather had become colder, and he knew that in a few minutes the damp pieces of ice would be firmly cemented together.

Hardly had he lifted the last piece to its place, when the pack came rushing about him, snapping and snarling, but at first not testing the strength of his intrenchment. When soon they began to spring against it, and snap at the corners of ice, the frost had done its work, and they could not loosen his hastily built wall.

Through narrow crevices he could look out at them, and at one time counted sixteen grouped together in council. As the cold increased he had to keep in motion in order not to freeze, and any extra action on his part increased the fierceness of the wolves. At times they would gather in a circle around him, and after sniffing at him eagerly, set up a doleful howling, as if deploring the excellent supper they had lost.

Ere long one of them found an opening at a corner large enough to admit its head; but Evan was on the alert, and gave it such a blow with the axe as to cause its death. Soon another tried the same thing, and met with the same reception, withdrawing and whirling around several times, and then dropping dead with a broken skull.

One smaller than the rest attempting to enter, and receiving the fatal blow, crawled, in its dying agony, completely into the enclosure, and lay dead at Evan's feet. Of this he was not sorry, as his feet were bitterly cold, and the warm carcass of the animal served to relieve them.

In the course of the night six wolves were killed as they sought to creep into his fortress, and several others so seriously hacked as to send them to the woods again; and, however correct the notion that when on the hunt they devour their fallen comrades, in this case they did no such thing, as in the morning the six dead bodies lay about on the ice, and Evan had the profitable privilege of taking off their skins.

Of his thoughts during the night, a quotation from his diary is quaintly suggestive and characteristic.

"I bethought me of the wars of Glendower, which I have read about, and the battle of Grosmont Castle; and I said, 'I am Owen Glendower; this is my castle; the wolves are the army of Henry; but I will never surrender or yield as did Glendower.'"

Toward morning, as the change of weather continued, and the waters of the river began to diminish, there was suddenly a prodigious crack and crash of the ice-bridge, and the whole mass settled several inches. At this the wolves took alarm, and in an instant fled. Perhaps they might have returned had not the crackling of the ice been repeated frequently.

At length Evan became alarmed for his safety, lest the ice should break up in the current, and bringing his axe to bear, soon burst his way out and fled to the shore. But not seeing the ice crumble, he ventured back to obtain the other axe, and then hastened home to his employer.

During the day he skinned the wolves, and within a fortnight pocketed the bounty money, amounting in all to about one hundred and fifty dollars. With this money he made the first payment on a large farm, which he long lived to cultivate and enjoy, and under the sod of which he found a quiet grave.

IRVING L. BEMAN.

HOW THEY BROUGHT THE GOOD NEWS
FROM GHENT TO AIX.

I sprang to the stirrup, and Joris and he:
I galloped, Dirck galloped, we galloped all three;
"Good speed!" cried the watch as the gate-bolts undrew,
"Speed!" echoed the wall to us galloping through.
Behind shut the postern, the lights sank to rest,
And into the midnight we galloped abreast.

Not a word to each other; we kept the great pace—
Neck by neck, stride by stride, never changing our place;
I turned in my saddle and made its girths tight,
Then shortened each stirrup and set the pique right,
Rebuckled the check-strap, chained slacker the bit,
Nor galloped less steadily Roland a whit.

'Twas moonset at starting; but while we drew near
Lokeren, the cocks crew and twilight dawned clear;
At Boom a great yellow star came out to see;
At Düffeld 'twas morning as plain as could be;
And from Mechlin church-steeple we heard the half-chime—
So Joris broke silence with "Yet there is time!"

At Aerschot up leaped of a sudden the sun,
And against him the cattle stood black every one,
To stare through the mist at us galloping past;
And I saw my stout galloper Roland at last
With resolute shoulders, each butting away
The haze, as some bluff river headland its spray;

And his low head and crest, just one sharp ear bent back
For my voice, and the other pricked out on his track,
And one eye's black intelligence—ever that glance

O'er its white edge at me, his own master, askance;
And the thick heavy spume-flakes, which aye and anon
His fierce lips shook upwards in galloping on.

By Hasselt, Dirck groaned; and cried Joris, "Stay spur!
Your Roos galloped bravely, the fault's not in her;
We'll remember at Aix"—for one heard the quick wheeze
Of her chest, saw the stretched neck and staggering knees,
And sunk tail, and horrible heave of the flank,
As down on her haunches she shuddered and sank.

So we were left galloping, Joris and I,
Past Looz and past Tongres, no cloud in the sky;
The broad sun above laughed a pitiless laugh;
'Neath our feet broke the brittle bright stubble like chaff;
Till over by Delhem a dome-spire sprung white,
And "Gallop," gasped Joris, "for Aix is in sight!

"How they'll greet us!" and all in a moment his roan
Rolled neck and croup over, lay dead as a stone;
And there was my Roland to bear the whole weight
Of the news which alone could save Aix from her fate,
With his nostrils like pits full of blood to the brim,
And with circles of red for his eye-sockets' rim.

Then I cast loose my buff-coat, each holster let fall,
Shook off both my jack-boots, let go belt and all,
Stood up in the stirrup, leaned, patted his ear,
Called my Roland his pet name, my horse without peer—
Clapped my hands, laughed and sung, any noise, bad or good,
Till at length into Aix, Roland galloped and stood.

And all I remember is friends flocking round,
As I sate with his head twixt my knees on the ground;
And no voice but was praising this Roland of mine
As I poured down his throat our last measure of wine,
Which (the burgesses voted by common consent)
Was no more than his due who brought good news from Ghent.

ROBERT BROWNING.

A HERO.

(*A Story of the American Revolution.*)

They were sitting by the great blazing wood-fire. It was July, but there was an east wind and the night was chilly. Besides, Mrs. Heath had a piece of fresh pork to roast. Squire Blake had "killed" the day before—that was the term used to signify the slaughter of any domestic animal for food—and had distributed the "fresh" to various families in town, and Mrs. Heath wanted hers for the early breakfast. Meat was the only thing to be had in plenty—meat and berries. Wheat and corn, and vegetables even, were scarce. There had been a long winter, and then, too, every family had sent early in the season all they could possibly spare to the Continental army. As to sugar and tea and molasses, it was many a day since they had had even the taste of them.

The piece of pork was suspended from the ceiling by a stout string, and slowly revolved before the fire, Dorothy or Arthur giving it a fresh start when it showed signs of stopping. There was a settle at right angles with the fireplace, and here the little cooks sat, Dorothy in the corner nearest the fire, and Arthur curled up on the floor at her feet, where he could look up the chimney and see the moon, almost at the full, drifting through the sky. At the opposite corner sat Abram, the hired man and faithful keeper of the family in the absence of its head, at work on an axe helve, while Bathsheba, or "Basha," as she was briefly and affectionately called, was spinning in one corner of the room just within range of the firelight.

There was no other light—the firelight being sufficient for their needs—and it was necessary to economize in candles, for any day a raid from the royal army might take away both cattle and sheep, and then where would the tallow come from for the annual fall candle-making? There was a rumor—Abram had brought it home that very day—that the royal army were advancing, and red coats might make their appearance in Hartland at any time. Arthur and Dorothy were talking about it, as they turned the roasting fork.

"Wish I was a man," said Arthur, glancing towards his mother, who was sitting in a low splint chair knitting stockings for her boy's winter wear. "I'd like to shoot a red coat."

"O Arty!" exclaimed Dorothy reproachfully; "you're always thinking of shooting! Now *I* should like to nurse a sick soldier and wait upon him. Poor soldiers! it was dreadful what papa wrote to mamma about them."

"Would you nurse a red coat?" asked Arthur, indignantly.

"Yes," said Dorothy. "Though of course I should rather, a great deal rather, nurse one of our own soldiers. But, Arty," continued the little elder sister, "papa says if we must fight, why, we must fight bravely, but that we can be brave without fighting."

"Well, I mean to be a hero, and heroes always fight. King Arthur fought. Papa said so. He and his knights fought for the Sangreal, and liberty is our Sangreal. I'm glad my name is Arthur, anyhow, for Arthur means noble and high," he said, lifting his bright boyish face with its steadfast blue eyes, and glancing again towards his mother. She gave an answering smile.

"I hope my boy will always be noble and high in thought and deed. But, as papa said, to be a hero one does not need to fight, at least, not to fight men. We can fight bad tempers and bad thoughts and cowardly impulses. They who fight these things successfully are the truest heroes, my boy."

"Ah, but mamma, didn't I hear you tell grandmamma how you were proud of your hero. That's what you called papa when General Montgomery wrote to you, with his own hand, how he drove back the enemy at the head of his men, while the balls were flying and the cannons roaring and flashing; and when his horse was shot under him how he struggled out and cheered on his men, on foot, and the bullets whizzed and the men fell all around him, and he wasn't hurt and"—Here the boy stopped abruptly and sprang impulsively forward, for his mother's cheek had suddenly grown pale.

"True grit!" remarked Abram to Basha, in an undertone, as she paused in her walk to and fro by the spinning-wheel to join a broken thread. "But there never was a coward yet, man or woman, 'mong the Heaths, an' I've known 'em off an' on these seventy year. Now there was ole Gineral Heath," he continued, holding up the axe helve and viewing it critically with one eye shut, "he was a marster hand for fightin'. Fit the Injuns 's though he liked it. That gun up there was his'n."

"Tell us about the 'sassy one,'" said Arthur, turning at the word gun.

"Youngster, 'f I've told yer that story once, I've told yer fifty times," said Abram.

"Tell it again," said the boy eagerly. "And take down the gun, too."

Abram got up as briskly as his seventy years and his rheumatism would permit, and took down the gun from above the mantel-piece. It was a very large one.

"Not quite so tall as the old Gineral himself," said Abram, "but a purty near to it. This gun is 'bout seven feet, an' yer gran'ther was seven feet two—a powerful built man. Wall, the Injuns had been mighty obstreperous 'long 'bout that time, burnin' the Widder Brown's house and her an' her baby a-hidin' in a holler tree near by, an' carryin' off critters an' bosses, an' that day yer gran'ther was after 'em with a posse o' men, an' what did that pesky Injun do but git up on a rock a quarter o' a mile off an' jestickerlate in an outrigerous manner, like a sarcy boy, an' yer grand'ther, he took aim and fired, an' that impident Injun jest tumbel over with a yell; his last, mind ye, and good enough for him!"

"I like to hear about old gran'ther," said Arthur.

As Abram was restoring the gun to its place upon the hooks, a sound was heard at the side door—a sound as of a heavy body falling against it, which startled them all. The dog Cæsar rose, and going to the door which opened into the side entry, sniffed along the crack above the threshold. Apparently satisfied, he barked softly, and rising on his hind legs lifted the latch and sprang into the entry. Abram followed with Basha. As he lifted the latch of the outer door—the string had been drawn in early, as was the custom in those troublous time—and swung it back, the light from the fire fell upon the figure of a man lying across the doorstone.

"Sakes alive!" exclaimed Abram, drawing back. But at a word from the mistress, they lifted the man and brought him in and laid him down on the braided woollen mat before the fire. Then for a moment there was silence, for he wore the dress of a British soldier, and his right arm was bandaged. He had fainted from loss of blood, apparently—perhaps from hunger. Basha loosened his coat at the throat, and tried to force a drop or two of "spirits" into his mouth, while Mrs. Heath rubbed his hands.

"He ain't dead," said Basha, in a grim tone, "and mind you, we'll see trouble from this." Basha was an arrant rebel, and hated the very sight of a red coat. "What are you doing here," she continued, addressing him, "killin' honest folks, when you'd better 've staid cross seas in yer own country?"

"Basha!" said Mrs. Heath reprovingly, "he is helpless."

But Basha as she unwound the tight bandage from the shattered arm, kept muttering to herself like a rising tempest, until at length the man having come quite to himself, detected her feeling, and with great effort said, "I am *not* a British soldier."

"Then what to goodness have you got on their uniform for?" queried Basha.

Little by little the pitiful story was told. He was an American soldier who had been doing duty as a spy in the British camp. Up to the very last day of his stay he had not been suspected; but trying to get away he was suspected, challenged, and fired at. The shot passed through his arm. He was certain his pursuers had followed him till night, and they would be likely to continue the search the next day, and he begged Mrs. Heath to secrete him for a day or two, if possible.

"I wouldn't mind being shot, marm," he said, "but you know they'll hang me if they get me. Of course I risked it when I went into their camp, but it's none the pleasanter for all that."

Now in the old Heath house there was a secret chamber, built in the side of the chimney. Most of those old colonial houses had enormous chimneys, that took up, sometimes, a quarter of the ground occupied by the house, so it was not a difficult thing to enclose a small space with slight danger of its existence being detected. This chimney chamber in the Heath house was little more than a closet eight feet by four. It was entered from the north chamber, Abram's room, through a narrow sliding panel that looked exactly like the rest of the wall, which was of cedar boards. An inch-wide shaft running up the side of the chimney ventilated the closet, and it was lighted by a window consisting of three small panes of glass carefully concealed under the projecting roof. In a sunny day one could see to read there easily.

A small cot-bed was now carried into this room, and up there, after his wound had been dressed by Basha, who, like many old-time women, was skilful in dressing wounds and learned in the properties of herbs and roots, and he had been fed and bathed, the soldier was taken; and a very grateful man he was as he settled himself upon the comfortable bed and looked up with a smiling "thank you," into Basha's face, which was no longer grim and forbidding.

All this time no special notice had been taken of Dorothy and Arthur. They had followed about to watch the bathing, feeding and tending, and when Mrs. Heath turned to leave the secret chamber, she found them behind her, staring in with very wide-open eyes indeed; for, if you can believe it, they never before had even heard of, much less seen, this lovely little secret chamber. It was never deemed wise in colonial families to talk about these hiding-places, which sometimes served so good a purpose, and I doubt if many adults in the town of Hartland knew of this secret chamber in the Heath house.

The panel was closed, and Abram was left to care for the wounded soldier through the night. It was nine o'clock, the colonial hour for going to bed, and long past the children's hour, and Dotty and Arthur in their prayers by their mother's knee, put up a petition for the safety of the stranger.

"*Would* they hang him if they could get him, mamma?" asked Arty.

"Certainly," she replied. "It is one of the rules of warfare. A spy is always hung."

In the morning, from nine to eleven, Mrs. Heath always devoted to the children's lessons. Arthur, who was eleven, was a good Latin scholar. He was reading *Cæsar's Commentaries,* and he liked it—that is, he liked the story part. He found some of it pretty tough reading, and I need not tell you boys who have read Cæsar, what parts those were. They had English readings from the *Spectator,* and from Bishop Leighton's works, books which you know but little about. Dotty had a daily lesson in botany, and very pleasant hours those school hours were.

After dinner, at twelve, they had the afternoon for play. That afternoon, the day after the soldier came, they went berrying. They did this almost every day during berry time, so as to have what they liked better than anything for supper —berries and milk. Occasionally they had huckleberry "slap-jacks," also a favorite dish, for breakfast; not often, however, as flour was scarce.

They went for berries down the road known as South Lane, a lonely place, but where berries grew plentifully. Their mother had cautioned them not to talk about the occurrence of the night before, as some one might overhear, and so, though they talked about their play and their studies, about papa and his soldiers, they said nothing about *the* soldier.

"Tell Me, My Little Man," Said He, "Where You Saw the British Uniform."

They had nearly filled their baskets, when a growl from Cæsar startled them, and turning, they saw two horsemen who had stopped near by, one of whom was just springing from his horse. They were in British uniform, and the children at once were sure what they wanted.

"O Arty, Arty!" whispered Dorothy. "They've come, and we mustn't tell."

The man advanced with a smile meant to be pleasant, but which was in reality so sinister that the children shrank with a sensation of fear.

"How are you, my little man? Picking berries, eh? And where do you live?" he asked.

"With mamma," answered Arthur promptly.

"And who is mamma? What is her name?"

"Mrs. Heath," said Arty.

"And don't you live with papa too? Where is papa?" the man asked.

Arthur hesitated an instant, and then out it came, and proudly too. "In the Continental army, sir."

"Ho! ho! and so we are a little rebel, are we?" laughed the man. "And who am I? Do you know?"

"Yes, sir; a British soldier."

"How do you know that?"

"Because you wear their uniform, sir?"

"You cannot have seen many British soldiers here," said the man. "Did you ever see the British uniform before?"

"Yes, sir," replied Arty.

"And where did you see it?" he asked, glancing sharply at Arthur and then at Dorothy. Upon the face of the latter was a look of dismay, for she had foreseen the drift of the man's questions and the trap into which Arty had fallen. He, too, saw it, now he was in. The only British uniform he had ever seen was that worn by the American spy. For a brief moment he was tempted to tell a lie. Then he said firmly, "I cannot tell you, sir."

"Cannot! Does that mean will not?" said the man threateningly. Then he put his hand into his pocket and took out a bright gold sovereign, which he held before Arthur.

"Come, now, my little man, tell me where you saw the British soldier's uniform, and you shall have this gold piece."

But all the noble impulses of the boy's nature, inherited and strengthened by his mother's teachings, revolted at this attempt to bribe him. His eyes flashed. He looked the man full in the face. "I will not!" said he.

"Come, come!" cried out the man on horseback. "Don't palter any longer with the little rebel. We'll find a way to make him tell. Up with him!"

In an instant the man had swung Arthur into his saddle, and leaping up behind him, struck spurs to his horse and dashed away. Cæsar, who had been sniffing about, suspicious, but uncertain, attempted to leap upon the horseman in the rear, but he, drawing his pistol from his saddle, fired, and Cæsar dropped helpless.

The horsemen quickly vanished, and for a moment Dorothy stood pale and speechless. Then she knelt down by Cæsar, examined his wound—he was shot in the leg—and bound it up with her handkerchief, just as she saw Basha do the night before, and then putting her arms around his neck she kissed him. "Be patient, dear old Cæsar, and Abram shall come for you!"

Covered with dust, her frock stained with Cæsar's blood, a pitiful sight indeed was Dorothy as she burst into the kitchen where Basha was preparing supper.

"O mamma, they've carried off Arty and shot Cæsar, those dreadful, dreadful British!"

Between her sobs she told the whole fearful story to the two women—fearful, I say, for Mrs. Heath knew too well the reputed character of the British soldiery, not to fear the worst if her boy should persist in refusing to tell where he had seen the British soldier's uniform. But even in her distress she was conscious of a proud faith that he would not betray his trust.

As to Basha, who shall describe her horror and indignation? "The wretches! ain't they content to murder our men and burn our houses, that they must take our innercent little boys?" and she struck the spit into the chicken she was preparing for supper vindictively, as though thus she would like to treat the whole British army. "The dear little cretur! what'll he do to-night without his mamma, and him never away from her a night in his blessed life. 'Pears to me the Lord's forgot the Colonies. O dearie, dearie me!" utterly overcome she dropped into a chair, and throwing her homespun check apron over her head, she gave way to such a fit of weeping as astonished and perplexed Abram, one of whose principal articles of faith it was that Basha couldn't shed a tear, even if she tried, "more'n if she's made o' cast iron."

It indeed looked hopeless. Who was to follow after these men and rescue Arthur? There was hardly any one left in town but old men, women and children.

Mrs. Heath thought of this as she soothed Dorothy, coaxed her to eat a little supper, and then sat by her side until she fell asleep. She sat by the fire while the embers died out, or walked up and down the long, lonely kitchen, wrestling, like Jacob, in prayer, for her boy, until long after midnight.

And now let us follow Arthur's fortunes. The men galloped hard and long over hills, through valleys and woods, so far away it seemed to the little fellow he could never possibly see mamma or Dorothy again. At last they drew up at a large white house, evidently the headquarters of the officers, and Arthur was put at once into a dark closet and there left. He was tired and dreadfully hungry, so hungry that he could think of hardly anything else. He heard the rattling of china and glasses, and knew they were at supper. By and by a servant came and took him into the supper room. His eyes were so dazzled at first by the change from the dark closet to the well-lighted room, that he could scarcely see. But when the daze cleared he found himself standing near the head of the table, where sat a stout man with a red face, a fierce mustache, and an evil pair of eyes.

He looked at Arthur a moment. Then he poured out a glass of wine and pushed it towards him: "Drink!"

But Arthur did not touch the glass.

"Drink, I say," he repeated impatiently. "Do you hear?"

"I have promised mamma never to drink wine," was the low response.

It seemed to poor Arthur as though everything had combined against him. It was bad enough to have to say no to the question about the uniform, and now here was something else that would make the men still more angry with him. But the officer did not push his command; he simply thrust the glass one side and said, "Now, my boy, we're going to get that American spy and hang him. You know where he is and you've got to tell us, or it will be the worse for you. Do you want to see your mother again?"

Arthur did not answer. He could not have answered just then. A big bunch came into his throat. Cry? Not before these men. So he kept silence.

"Obstinate little pig! speak!" thundered the officer, bringing his great brawny fist down upon the table with a blow that set the glasses dancing. "Will you tell me where that spy is?"

"No, sir," came in very low, but very firm tones. I will not tell you the dreadful words of that officer, as he turned to his servant with the command, "Put him down cellar, and we'll see to him in the morning. They're all alike, men, women and children. Rebellion in the very blood. The only way to finish it is to spill it without mercy."

Now there was one thing that Arthur, brave as he was, feared, and that was— rats! Left on a heap of dry straw, he began to wonder if there were rats there. Presently he was sure he heard something move, but he was quickly reassured by the touch of soft, warm fur on his hand, and the sound of a melodious "pur-r." The friendly kitty, glad of a companion, curled herself by his side. What comfort she brought to the lonely little fellow! He lay down beside her, and saying his *Our Father*, and *Now I Lay Me*, was soon in a profound sleep, the purring little kitty nestling close.

The sounds of revelry in the rooms above did not disturb him. The boisterous songs and laughter, the stamping of many feet, continued far into the night. At last they ceased; and when everything had been for a long time silent, the door leading to the cellar was softly opened and a lady came down the stairway. I have often wished that I might paint her as she looked coming down those stairs. Arthur was afterwards my great-grandfather, you know, and he told me this story when I was a young girl in my teens. He told me how lovely this lady was.

Her gown was of some rich stuff that shimmered in the light of the candle she carried, and rustled musically as she walked. There was a flash of jewels at her throat and on her hands. She had wrapped a crimson mantle about her head and shoulders. Her eyes were like stars on a summer's night, sparkling with a veiled radiance, and as she stood and looked down upon the sleeping boy, a smile, sweet, but full of a profound sadness, played upon her lips. Then a determined look came into her bright eyes.

He stirred in his sleep, laughed out, said "mamma," and then opened his eyes. She stooped and touched his lips with her finger. "Hush! Speak only in a whisper. Eat this, and then I will take you to your mother."

After he had eaten, she wrapped a cloak about him, and together they stole up and out past the sleeping, drunken sentinel, to the stables. She lead out a white horse, her own horse, Arthur was sure, for the creature caressed her with his head, and as she saddled him she talked to him in low tones, sweet, musical words of some foreign tongue. The handsome horse seemed to understand the necessity of silence, for he did not even whinny to the touch of his mistress' hand, and trod daintily and noiselessly as she led him to the mounting block, his small ears pricking forward and backward, as though knowing the need of watchful listening.

Leaping to the saddle and stooping, she lifted Arthur in front of her, and with a word they were off. A slow walk at first, and then a rapid canter. Arthur never forgot that long night ride with the beautiful lady on the white horse, over the country flooded with the brilliancy of the full moon. Once or twice she asked him if he was cold, as she drew the cloak more closely about him, and sometimes she would murmur softly to herself words in that silvery, foreign tongue. As they drew near Hartland, she asked him to point out his father's house, and when they were quite near, only a little distance off, she stopped the horse.

"I leave you here, you brave, darling boy," she said. "Kiss me once, and then jump down. And don't forget me."

Arthur threw his arms around her neck and kissed her, first on one cheek and then on the other, and looking up into the beautiful face with its starry eyes, said:

"I will never, never forget you, for you are the loveliest lady I ever saw—except mamma."

She laughed a pleased laugh, like a child, then took a ring from her hand and put it on one of Arthur's fingers. Her hand was so slender it fitted his chubby little hand very well.

"Keep this," she said, "and by and by give it to some lady good and true, like mamma."

"Will you be punished?" he said, keeping her hand. She laughed again, with a proud, daring toss of her dainty head, and rode away.

Arthur watched her out of sight, and then turned towards home. Mrs. Heath was still keeping her lonely watch, when the latch of the outer door was softly lifted—nobody had the heart to take in the string with Arty outside—the inner door swung noiselessly back, and the blithe voice said, "Mamma! mamma! here I am, and I didn't tell."

All that day, and the next, and the next, the Heath household were in momentary expectation of the coming of the red coats to search for the spy. Dorothy and Arthur, and sometimes Abram, did picket duty to give seasonable warning of their approach. But they never came. In a few days news was brought that the British forces, on the very morning after Arthur's return, had made a rapid retreat before an advance of the Federal troops, and never again was a red coat seen in Hartland. The spy got well in great peace and comfort under Basha's nursing, and went back again to do service in the Continental army, and Dotty used to say, "You did learn, didn't you, Arty, how a person, even a little boy, can be a hero without fighting, just as mamma said?"

Teddy the Teazer

by M.E.B.

A Moral Story with a Velocipede Attachment

Teddy the Teazer

A Moral Story with a Velocipede Attachment

He wanted a velocipede,
   And shook his saucy head;
He thought of it in daytime,
   He dreamed of it in bed,
He begged for it at morning,
   He cried for it at noon,
And even in the evening
   He sang the same old tune.

He wanted a velocipede!
   It was no use to say
He was too small to manage it,
   Or it might run away,
Or crack his little occiput,
   Or break his little leg—
It made no bit of difference,
   He'd beg, and beg, and beg.

He wanted a velocipede,
   A big one with a gong
To startle all the people,
   As they saw him speed along;
A big one, with a cushion,
   And painted red and black,
To make the others jealous
   And clear them off the track.

He wanted a velocipede,
   The largest ever built,
Though he was only five years old
   And wore a little kilt,
And hair in curls a-waving,

And sashes by his side,
And collars wide as cart-wheels,
    Which hurt his manly pride!

He wanted a velocipede
    With springs of burnished steel;
He knew the way to work it—
    The treadle for the wheel,
The brake to turn and twist it,
    The crank to make it stop,
My! hadn't he been riding
    For days, with Jimmy Top?

He wanted a velocipede!
    Why, he was just as tall
As six-year-old Tom Tucker,
    Who wasn't very small!
And feel his muscle, will you?
    And tell him, if you dare,
That he's the sort of fellow
    To get a fall, or scare?

They got him a velocipede;
    I really do not know
How they could ever do it,
    But then, he teased them so,
And so abused their patience,
    And dulled their nerves of right,
That they just lost their senses
    And brought it home one night.

They bought him a velocipede—
    O woe the day and hour!
When proudly seated on it,
    In pomp of pride and power,
His foot upon the treadle,
    With motion staid and slow
He turned upon his axle,
    And made the big thing go.

Alas, for the velocipede!
    The way ran down a hill—
The whirling wheels went faster,
    And fast, and faster still,
Until, like flash of rocket,
    Or shooting star at night,
They crossed the dim horizon
    And rattled out of sight.

So vanished the velocipede,
    With him who rode thereon;
And no one, since that dreadful day,
    Has found out where 'tis gone!
Except a floating rumor
    Which some stray wind doth blow.
When the long nights of winter
    Are white with frost and snow,
Of a small fleeting shadow,
    That seems to run astray
Upon a pair of flying wheels,
    Along the Milky Way.

And this they think is Teddy!
    Doomed for all time to speed—
A wretched little phantom boy,
    On a velocipede!

M.E.B.

JOJO'S PETITION.

Golden-haired Jojo, at his mother's knee,
　　Nestles each night his baby prayer to say:
"Bless papa and mamma! make Ned and me
　　Good little boys!" he has been taught to pray.

Grandmamma was very sick one weary day,
　　And Jojo shared with us our anxious care;
So the dear child, when he knelt down to pray,
　　Seemed to think Grandma must be in his prayer.

And sure the dear Lord did not fail to hear
　　Sharer alike of sorrows and of joys—
When he said, "Bless papa and my mamma dear,
　　And make me an' Gran'ma an' Neddy good boys!"

RUTH HALL.

Milton Keynes UK
Ingram Content Group UK Ltd.
UKHW050620080324
438959UK00012B/454